"Let me be

"The only reason you're still alive, Missy, is we need that stash." Gemma felt a sharp pain as he stepped down hard on her shoulder, and she yelped. "But we will do anything it takes to get it, even if it means tearing you limb from limb!"

Help...me...Lord...

A burst of furious barking filled the air. Simcoe? Footsteps pelted through the snow. Then a strong, unmistakable voice reached her ears.

"Leave her alone!"

It was Patrick.

He was coming for her and he wasn't going to let them take her.

Gemma still couldn't see anything in the pitch-black darkness that surrounded her. The sound of barking turned into a furious snarl. Her attacker swore loudly and the pressure suddenly left her arm. Then a crack split the air. Umber's voice stopped. And she felt the ground shift as Patrick knelt down beside her.

"It's okay," he said. "I'm here. You're safe now."

USA TODAY bestselling author **Maggie K. Black** is an award-winning journalist and self-defense instructor. She's lived in the United States, Europe and the Middle East, and left a piece of her heart in each. She now makes her home in Canada, where she writes stories that make her heart race.

Books by Maggie K. Black

Love Inspired Suspense

Undercover Protection
Surviving the Wilderness
Her Forgotten Life
Cold Case Chase
Undercover Baby Rescue

Unsolved Case Files

Cold Case Tracker
Christmas Cold Case
Dangerous Arson Trail
Christmas Under Threat

Mountain Country K-9 Unit

Crime Scene Secrets

Dakota K-9 Unit

Cold Case Peril

Visit the Author Profile page at LoveInspired.com for more titles.

CHRISTMAS UNDER THREAT

MAGGIE K. BLACK

If you purchased this book without a cover you should be aware that this book is stolen property. It was reported as "unsold and destroyed" to the publisher, and neither the author nor the publisher has received any payment for this "stripped book."

ISBN-13: 978-1-335-95740-5

Christmas Under Threat

Copyright © 2025 by Mags Storey

All rights reserved. No part of this book may be used or reproduced in any manner whatsoever without written permission.

Without limiting the author's and publisher's exclusive rights, any unauthorized use of this publication to train generative artificial intelligence (AI) technologies is expressly prohibited.

This is a work of fiction. Names, characters, places and incidents are either the product of the author's imagination or are used fictitiously. Any resemblance to actual persons, living or dead, businesses, companies, events or locales is entirely coincidental.

For questions and comments about the quality of this book, please contact us at CustomerService@Harlequin.com.

® is a trademark of Harlequin Enterprises ULC.

Love Inspired
22 Adelaide St. West, 41st Floor
Toronto, Ontario M5H 4E3, Canada
www.LoveInspired.com

Printed in Lithuania

The angel of the Lord encampeth round about them
that fear him, and delivereth them.
—*Psalm* 34:7

To all the incredible voice actors
who make these stories come alive in audiobooks.

And to all of you who hear the characters' voices
in your head as you read.

These stories may start in my mind,
but they come alive in yours.

ONE

The isolated diner, on the side of Highway 11 in Northern Ontario, twinkled and shone in a mishmash of colored lights and spinning silver foil window decorations, like it was fighting a defiant battle for Christmas joy against the cold gray slush that smacked the ground around it. Private detective Gemma Locke pulled her hatchback to stop in a well-lit corner of the lot and tucked a wisp of dark hair behind her ears. Then she turned to the brown and tan dog in the K-9 vest that sat smartly on the passenger seat behind her.

"Alright, Simcoe," she said to the Australian kelpie, "time to find out what Patrick knows."

Then she took a deep breath, whispered a prayer for wisdom and braced herself for what was about to be the trickiest and most important interview of her career. Interviews were part and parcel of the job, but this one felt different—the mother of this man's son had been murdered a decade ago. The Noëlville Serial Killer had terrorized small towns in Northern Ontario for twelve years, leaving seven different bodies lying in the forest along Highway 11. All leads had gone cold. So the Ontario police commissioner had taken the unprecedented step of handing the entire investigation over to her Cold Case Task Force to reinvestigate from the very beginning.

This had led them to a shocking and unexpected discovery—the first victim, found over a decade ago, was Patrick Craft's ex-girlfriend Lucy and the mother of his son, Tristan. Patrick was a handsome thirty-two-year-old single father, who owned a construction company on Manitoulin Island, served as the local fire chief and had helped her team solve a cold case last Christmas.

Now it was Gemma's job to break it to him before the media got hold of the news in a couple of days. But it also meant finding out what he'd thought of Lucy and her disappearance, before he discovered that she'd been a victim of a serial killer, which could change how he remembered things. Death had a way of brushing a layer of kindness and forgiveness over bad memories, and in her experience, most people knew far more about the mysteries around them than they ever realized. They just needed someone like her to help unlock the clues they'd ignored and the facts they'd forgotten.

She exited her vehicle and walked around to the passenger door, where the dog waited patiently as Gemma clipped her leash on. Simcoe was the first dog she'd ever lived with. Up to this point she'd just had a bird named Reepi, who was currently staying with a friend in Toronto. A cold wind nipped Gemma's skin. She wrapped her blue scarf tighter around her neck. A blizzard was scheduled to move in tonight that was forecast to dump almost two feet of snow in a few hours.

"Ever taken part in questioning a witness?" she asked Simcoe. "Gotta say, this is my first with a sidekick."

Simcoe barked in response. It was a confident sound, as if the dog knew exactly what was going on and was eager to help. Gemma smiled and watched as the dog leaped out gingerly, landing on her three legs. Then she bent over and attached a red bow to her collar. Simcoe had an intelligent face and alert, oversize ears that came up to Gemma's knee.

Truth was, she'd never really been a fan of dogs, despite the fact there were several truly wonderful K-9s on the team. But when her boss, Inspector Ethan Finnick, had brought the three-legged dog into their North Toronto offices, and told them that she'd lost a limb saving the lives of two kidnapped children from a fire—after Simcoe's former human partner had cowardly turned tail and run—Gemma was immediately on her feet offering to give the dog a home.

Together, Gemma and Simcoe made their way across the parking lot. Her blue eyes scanned the scene. There were a handful of people in the diner, but it was hard to see much of anything past the flurry of decorations covering the windows. Four other cars in the lot—two of which looked far too expensive to be parked outside an out-of-the-way joint like this—along with Patrick's white Craft and Son Construction van. The cell signal on her phone was worryingly weak. The clock told her it was fourteen minutes to seven, but the world was so gloomy it might as well be midnight. Then again, today was December 22, statistically the second darkest day of the year,

She was about ten feet away from the door when she heard Simcoe growl.

Gemma froze. It was a low, warning sound that came from the back of the dog's throat. The kelpie sniffed the air, and Gemma suddenly realized that the K-9 was alerting. Simcoe sensed that something was wrong and was waiting for the instruction to pursue it. The sense of approaching danger prickled at the nape of Gemma's neck.

Lord, help me see what I need to see.

Simcoe was cross-trained in drug detection and search and rescue, and since the K-9 hadn't been told to find anyone, she was clearly detecting drugs, and at a volume the dog couldn't tune out. Gemma turned as something moved in the shadows, just out of the corner of her eye.

It was a woman.

She was a few inches taller than Gemma's five-foot-two frame and thin, with her face entirely shrouded in the hood of her jacket. Gemma watched as the woman ducked her head and darted furtively between the cars, like she was trying to search them for something without being noticed.

Was she checking for Christmas gifts left on the seats, for a quick smash and grab? The diner was on the side of a rural highway, miles from anywhere. But she was definitely looking for something. Or someone.

"Hey," Gemma called to her. "Are you okay? Do you need help?"

The woman startled and then dashed around the side of the diner. Seconds later Gemma heard the engine of a badly maintained vehicle roar. The jalopy disappeared down Highway 11. Gemma filed the incident away in her mental filing cabinet of suspicious incidents, then she strode to the diner and pushed open the door.

A blast of Christmas music hit her like a gale force wind. Paper chains danced about her head. The branches of an artificial Christmas tree brushed against her sleeves as she walked forward and let the door close behind her.

"Just seat yourself, hon!" a blonde waitress called cheerfully from behind a red-and-white-tiled counter. "Can I get you anything?"

The waitress was the type of pretty that came from smiling a lot. Late forties but could pass for a decade younger.

"Hot chocolate would be great," Gemma said.

"Coming right up."

"Thanks."

Gemma's mind hummed like a well-tuned machine as she

took in the scene. Whatever scent Simcoe had been concerned about outside, the kelpie didn't seem to be detecting it now. To her right, an elderly couple sat together in the first booth. Their hands touched, in comfortable silence. Behind them sat three well-dressed men in fedoras and matching wool trench coats, each in a slightly different shade of light brown. Umber, bone and rust, she noted, all designer shades. The three men looked as out of place in the diner as the expensive cars had in the lot. Everything about them screamed "private security."

Then she spotted Patrick Craft sitting with his son in a corner booth, half-hidden behind the counter. She blinked. Oh. She hadn't expected Patrick to bring his kid with him. That would complicate things. She imagined Patrick would want to tell Tristan about his mother's death in his own time and in his own way, and not hear it from her. When she'd called Patrick that morning and asked if they could meet up and talk—it was the kind of conversation best had in person—she was surprised and thankful when he'd said he was in Huntsville for the day and could meet her on his way back to the island. She had a cottage barely thirty minutes away on Cedar Lake, which she was staying in over the holidays. Then it was only a matter of finding a place on the highway that welcomed dogs.

Neither Patrick nor his son noticed her at first. The preteen's eyes were locked on a portable LMNTL game device. Pronounced "elemental," the company was world-famous for its expensive children's toys. Tristan was a skinny kid with a mop of blond hair and brows that were knit in frustration, either at the game he was playing, the patchy Wi-Fi connection or possibly both.

She stepped forward, and finally her gaze alighted at the tall and broad-shouldered man sitting across from the boy. Patrick had unzipped his heavy plaid winter coat, showing the open denim shirt and white T-shirt underneath. His short blond hair was tousled, like he'd run his fingers through it after taking off a toque and he had an impressive, yet rugged, moustache.

There was half of a large plate of fries on the table in front of him.

He looked up, she locked eyes with Patrick, and suddenly she felt her well-controlled world rock on its axis, as if the diner itself had tipped on its side. Her heart raced. Heat rose to her cheeks.

She'd forgotten how incredibly handsome he was.

Not that it mattered. She was here as a member of the Cold Case Task Force. This meeting was strictly professional. The fact he might possibly be the finest looking man she'd ever seen in her life didn't matter. And even if this hadn't been a work meeting, she was too committed to her work to even consider a romantic relationship with anyone. Not to mention, too independent.

Patrick stood slowly, and for a long moment he didn't say anything. He didn't smile either. Instead, she watched as a question formed in the depths of his eyes, and she suddenly remembered that this man had once been falsely accused of committing a terrible crime he'd definitely been innocent of. Was he suspicious of her reason for wanting to meet? She wouldn't exactly blame him if he was.

"Gemma, right?" he asked, with a professional smile. He stuck his hand out to shake hers. "I'm Patrick Craft. This is my son, Tristan."

"Nice to see you again," she said, reaching a hand out. "Thanks for coming."

His hand enveloped hers. The handshake was warm and strong, and just the right amount of firm. "How was the drive up? It's like three hours from the city right?"

By "the city," he meant Toronto.

"More or less," Gemma confirmed. "Thankfully, I have a small cottage not that far away. I used to live up here full-time, but I moved to Toronto when I joined the task force. Basically I'm a city girl at heart."

"Good for some, I guess," Patrick said, shrugging. "I couldn't ever imagine living hemmed in by all those buildings. Considering how quickly that storm seems to be coming in, I just hope we make it back to the island before they close the swing bridge or we'll be stuck on the mainland overnight. You heard they're forecasting two feet?"

Patrick whistled and Gemma nodded. She'd need to watch the time during their conversation.

"Yeah," she said. "That's a lot, even for here."

"Oh, cool, you brought a dog!" Tristan leaped from his seat and dropped down beside Simcoe. The dog's tail thumped the floor as the boy scratched her behind the ears. "Why does she only have three legs?"

Suddenly, Gemma realized she still hadn't let go of Patrick's hand. She quickly pulled it away and tucked it in the crook of the opposite elbow. Her skin was tingling.

"Simcoe was injured in the line of duty," she said. "She ran into a burning building to find some children who'd been kidnapped and alerted the firefighters to a hidden door to find them. She's a hero."

"Wow." Tristan ran both hands through the kelpie's fur.

Patrick looked down at his son. "Kiddo, I think Officer Locke was hoping to talk to me alone." He glanced at her face as if searching for confirmation. Then before she could say anything, he turned back to Tristan. "Why don't you take your game thingy, and go sit in the booth by the tree, with your headphones on?"

"Okay," Tristan said, cheerfully. He gave the dog one more

pat and then straightened up. She sat and so did Patrick. She unzipped her jacket, but like Patrick, she didn't take it off. He pushed the plate of fries toward her.

"Help yourself," he said. "I wasn't sure if you'd be hungry, so I ordered extra in case."

"Thank you." She popped one in her mouth, more out of curiosity than hunger. It was wonderfully salty and crisp. Simcoe slipped under the table and curled up by her feet. "You can call me Gemma, by the way. I'm not an officer. In fact, I'm the only one on the Cold Case Task Force who isn't. I'm a private eye." He looked genuinely interested, so she went on. "A lot of cold cases are caused because police bungled the initial investigation," Gemma said, "or the fact that sometimes the people who do have important information won't come forward because they don't want to get in trouble with the police, like former criminals. My role is to help get through to those people who don't trust the cops on my team, and convince them that we're all in this together."

The waitress set a mug of hot chocolate in front of her and left. The mug was red and the hot chocolate had mini marshmallows.

She wrapped her hands around it and felt the warmth in her palms.

"So, what's this about?" He batted the question across the table to her as lightly and breezily as a Ping-Pong ball. But she could still catch the undercurrent of worry and concern floating under the words, as if he was both sizing her up and getting the necessary chat out of the way before they got down to the real reason Gemma had asked him to meet on the highway three days before Christmas.

"It's been a little over a year now since my boss, Inspector Ethan Finnick, was tasked with putting together a team to investigate cold cases that was completely independent from other law enforcement divisions." He nodded as if to show he was following. "Right now, Finnick's got the whole team working on the Noëlville Serial Killer case. Have you heard of it?"

"Seven bodies wrapped in plastic dumped in the forest between North Bay, Sudbury and Noëlville?" Patrick asked. "All found around Christmas?"

"Yeah," she said, "over the span of twelve years. But only a few of the Noëlville Serial Killer's victims were killed before they were dumped. Most died of exposure after being left in the woods, injured and wrapped up in plastic. Also, they weren't all found at Christmas."

A gust of cold air sent chills down the back of her neck. The elderly couple were on their way out. The men in brown coats and fedoras were paying their bill with cash. She turned back and took a sip of her hot chocolate. It was surprisingly good.

"With a serial killer like that," she went on, "it's all about creating fear. The Noëlville Serial Killer has been built up as this terrifying, larger-than-life monster. To make a long story short, all leads had gone cold, and there was a public outcry about the lack of the progress law enforcement were making, so the Ontario police commissioner asked our task force to take over the case and reinvestigate it from the beginning. Finnick actually thinks there might not be one single serial killer but multiple, who may or may not be connected."

She'd fill Patrick in more about the investigation later if he wanted details, but right now, that summed up the basics that he needed to know. She took a deep breath and braced herself. "Does the name Marissa Kerry mean anything to you?"

Patrick shook his head. "No, should it?"

"She was the Noëlville Serial Killer's first victim," Gemma

said. "At least that's who law enforcement always believed because the body was found with Marissa's wallet."

Until the Cold Case Task Force reopened the investigation, reexamined the evidence, ran a fresh DNA search and found a match in the last place they'd ever expected—a sample of Tristan's DNA that was taken during routine evidence collection last year while they were working on another case. It was a missing persons case of a young student on Manitoulin Island, which the task force concluded had been a murder...at the hands of Patrick's best friend. Patrick had been instrumental in finding and retrieving Stella Neilson's body. Tristan, whose prints had been on some evidence, had been ruled out, but his sample was in the system. Which was how they'd discovered that the Noëlville Serial Killer's first victim, whom law enforcement had mistakenly been calling Marissa all this time, was really Patrick's ex and the mother of his son—Lucy Marsh.

She took a deep breath. *Lord, guide my words.*

"You have to understand," she continued, "police didn't have a DNA profile for Marissa Kerry to compare the victim against when she was discovered over a decade ago. Because the body matched Marissa's description, she was carrying her wallet and she was a troubled woman and drug user, law enforcement just assumed—"

"Dad, I'm going to go wash my hands," Tristan called as he approached their table.

Patrick turned and looked at his son. A sign for the washrooms hung above a hallway to their left. "Yeah, sure. Just come right back when you're done."

"Okay!" Tristan left his jacket in the booth and started down the hall.

Patrick watched him go for a long moment.

How would he take the news that Tristan's mother was dead? How would Tristan take it?

"You've raised Tristan on your own, right?" she asked.

"Ever since he was six months old," Patrick said.

She searched his face for any flicker of emotion as he said that, but it remained steadily calm.

"Can I ask what happened to his mom?" Gemma asked.

Just like that, Patrick's jaw clenched. He crossed his arms across his chest and leaned back.

"I don't think that's any of your business," Patrick began. Then, as she watched, he seemed to catch himself. His eyes closed, he blew out a hard breath, and she had the distinct impression he was praying. Then he opened his eyes again and, while he still looked tense, he didn't seem quite as defensive. "Sorry, Tristan's mom—Lucy—has been out of our lives for a very, very long time." He let out a breath, shaking his head. "I was pretty surprised when Lucy reached out to me a few weeks ago."

An icy cold shiver ran down her limbs. Lucy Marsh had been dead for over a decade. She'd been murdered by a serial killer. Her body had been found wrapped in plastic in the forest.

So, who has Patrick been talking to?

And why were they pretending to be Lucy?

"Lucy reached out to you?" Gemma asked. "How? Why? What did she want?"

Patrick blinked.

"She emailed me," he said. "She said she'd seen my name in the news after I'd helped your task force, felt bad for depriving Tristan of a mother and wanted to make it up to him."

"Did you let her communicate with Tristan?" she asked.

"No—"

"Have you talked to her on the phone?"

"No—"

"Have you seen this before?" She pulled a folded piece of paper from her pocket and slid it across the table.

Patrick picked it up, unfolded it and looked down at the simple crude drawing of a bell. His face paled. "What's the meaning of this? What's going on?"

"So, you've seen it?"

"Lucy got this tattooed on her ankle because Tristan was born on Christmas."

"Law enforcement withheld this from the public for the sake of their investigation," Gemma said. "But all of the Noëlville Serial Killer's victims had this bell tattooed on them."

"What?" Patrick's mouth opened, but no words came out. Gemma reached across the table and grabbed his hands in hers.

"I'm sorry," she said, "but whoever you've been talking to isn't Tristan's mother. Lucy Marsh was killed by the Noëlville Serial Killer twelve years ago."

Patrick leaped to his feet, wrenching his hands away from hers. For a moment he just stared at her, as if his mouth was struggling to find anything to say. Then his eyes darted past her to the booth by the Christmas tree.

"Tristan hasn't come back from washing his hands," he said. The booth where his son had been sitting was empty except for Tristan's backpack and coat. Patrick rushed to the doorway that led to the washrooms. "Hey, Tristan!" he called. "You about done?"

For a moment he vanished from view and when he reappeared any last bit of color was gone from his face.

"Bathroom's empty. Tristan's gone!"

Gemma stood, but before she could speak, she heard a muffled shout.

Then the sound of a gunshot shook the air.

* * *

Panic rose inside Patrick's core as the noise rocked the night. Where was his son? Was he okay?

He ran down the hallway, passed the empty bathroom and burst through a side door into the darkness. Freezing rain beat down on the metal garbage cans. The lingering echo of the single gunshot seemed to be coming from all directions at once.

"Tristan!" he desperately shouted into the wind. Then he heard a dog barking and footsteps charging toward him. He glanced back in time to see Simcoe shoot past him. Gemma was five steps behind the K-9 carrying Tristan's coat.

"She's tracking him?" Patrick asked.

"I think so." Worry filled Gemma's blue eyes, and she ran a hand through her short dark hair. "Finnick's been training me to give Simcoe some basic orders."

Good enough for him. Patrick sprinted after the dog, with Gemma just a breath behind. Together they ran around the side of the diner. Simcoe's barks rose. Then he heard the dog snarl and a man yelp in a mixture of anger or fear. A second later they rounded the corner to see a tall man in a reddish-beige overcoat pinned against the brick wall, with Simcoe clamped on his arm and a fedora lying in the mud by his feet.

"Dad!" Tristan barreled from the darkness and into his father's chest.

"It's okay." Patrick wrapped his arms around his son protectively and held him to his side. "I'm here now. Are you hurt?"

"No, I'm fine." Tristan hugged him tightly.

"Simcoe!" Gemma called. "Release!"

The dog let go and wagged her tail as she promptly retreated to Gemma's side. But Gemma's keen eyes were focused on the ground. He could tell she was searching for something and within a second it seemed she'd found it. A handgun lay on the ground still smoking from where it had been fired. She dove for it. But the other man reached the gun first, wrapped his fingers around the grip and leaped up. In an instant, the world froze as the man raised the weapon. Gemma's hands rose to shoulder height and she stepped back. Simcoe growled. Patrick pushed his son behind him as prayers for help filled his heart. Anger flashed in the strange man's eyes as his gaze darted from Simcoe, to Tristan, to the trees beyond.

Then the man laughed self-consciously and slid his gun somewhere inside his overcoat, where it disappeared.

"Oops, sorry to scare you folks!" He held up his empty leather-gloved palms. "Kid here was startled by a bear in the woods, and I was just trying to scare it off. Isn't that right, kid?"

Patrick looked down at his son. "Is that true?"

"Yeah, Dad," Tristian said. "I'm so sorry. I came out for a better Wi-Fi signal, then I was scared by this bear, and this man shot at it."

His son was shivering and somehow looked younger than he had in a long time. But besides that he seemed to be okay. Freezing rain was still falling down around them, but Patrick's heart was pumping too hard to even notice the cold. Wordlessly, Gemma handed Tristan his jacket. He wriggled into it.

"A bear in December?" Gemma murmured, almost under her breath. "Bears don't usually leave hibernation until the spring."

Patrick glanced from his son's face over his head to Gemma, who now had her hand on Simcoe's collar. Her brow furrowed, and Patrick could tell in a glance that the private investigator was having trouble buying the story. As for himself, his father-heart was still churning with so many emotions it was like he'd just stepped off a carnival ride. He'd barely even begun to process the news that Lucy was dead, before he'd discovered Tristan was missing. Let alone the fact that someone had been impersonating Lucy, writing to him and trying to build a relationship with his son.

And sending Tristan expensive gifts.

In between the shock of learning that Lucy was dead and the scrambled rush to find Tristan, he'd neglected to tell Gemma about the presents that the Lucy imposter had sent, which were now stashed in the back of his garage.

Now a strange man had fired a gun near his son.

"That's quite the dog you've got there," the man said, turning to Gemma. He picked up his fedora, brushed it off and set it back on his head. "You're fortunate it didn't pierce the skin. I'd hate to have to take action against you."

Gemma faced the man head-on. He towered over her by more than a foot.

"Oh, she was just trying to stop you from firing that handgun of yours," she said. "She's too well trained to actually attack without knowing she has to."

"I hope so." The man smiled like an animal baring its teeth. "Because, it would be pretty sad for a boy to lose his dog over Christmas."

Fire flashed bright in the PI's eyes, but as Patrick watched, it was like he could almost see her biting back the words that were about to fly across her tongue. Instead, she glanced up to the dark skies above—like she was thinking or praying quickly—and when she looked back at the man an entirely new expression had brushed over her features. She looked surprised, almost apologetic.

"Oh, you must be a cop!" Gemma explained. Her sudden switch in tone had to be a PI tactic, and yet her wide-eyed wonder was so impressive that Patrick almost believed it was real. "I'm so sorry, Officer! For some reason, I thought you and your colleagues were private security. How do we report a bear sighting? Is there someone we should call? What type of bear was it?"

The man stepped back. Then he chuckled.

"Oh, I wouldn't worry about it," he said. "Truth is, I didn't get a good look at the animal. I was just talking on the phone when I heard this lad yelp. I came running to make sure he was okay and saw something rustling in the bushes. For all I know it was a big racoon. I'm thinking it's best we let this one go, for the sake of the boy and his dog." He tipped his hat. "You folks have a happy holiday."

He disappeared around the corner. Gemma's fake smile faded just as suddenly as it had appeared. She whispered a prayer of thanksgiving under her breath. Then she turned to Patrick.

"Well, that was fishy," she muttered. "If that man's a cop then I'm a ham sandwich. I'll meet with you inside. I'm pretty sure the waitress has already called 911. I'm going to try to get his license plate."

"Okay."

Gemma and Simcoe disappeared back around the corner. Patrick looked down at his son.

"I thought it was illegal to carry a gun like that in Canada," Tristan said.

"Pretty much," Patrick said. "It's very difficult to get a license to carry a handgun like that. It's possible he's private security, but even cops can't carry concealed without special permission."

"So, that guy broke the law?"

His son sounded genuinely curious, and Patrick couldn't

figure out whether to laugh or yell at him for terrifying him like that.

"Probably," Patrick said. But right now, what mattered most was keeping his son safe and getting him home. He steered Tristan back around the side of the building. "What are you doing outside, and why aren't you wearing your coat?"

"I wanted to finish my level and couldn't get a good internet signal," Tristan said. "I thought if I walked around it might be better."

Which was incredibly foolish but also something Patrick would imagine the preteen doing. He'd become pretty addicted to the game recently. Still, he couldn't shake the doubts about the story Gemma had voiced. "Is there something you're not telling me?"

"No!" Tristan's voice rose. "I was looking at my game, then I heard rustling and I kind of yelled. Then this man comes running around the corner and he shoots. Then almost immediately after Simcoe jumped on him."

"And you saw this bear?"

"No," Tristan said. "I mean, I just saw something moving in the bushes, and I think it was a bear. It all happened so fast I'm not really sure. After the man fired the gun, he turned to me and said something like, 'You're alright kid. It was just a bear, but I shot at the bear and now the bear's gone'."

Which could've been the truth, but it also sounded like the man was intentionally drilling the bear story into his son. But why? They reached the back door and stepped into the hallway of the diner. Women's voices trickled through from the main dining area. Patrick paused and placed a hand on Tristan's shoulder.

"You're not in trouble," he said. "But I need you to be totally honest with me. Did the man threaten you or point his gun at you—even if it was only for a second?"

He waited. But Tristan shook his head. "No, he only pointed it away from me and at the bear."

Which might or might not have been a bear. Or anything at all.

They walked into the dining room to find that Gemma and Simcoe had beaten them there. They must've sprinted around the building and in the front door. Gemma was talking to the waitress, but as he approached, the waitress excused herself and popped through the double doors into the kitchen. Gemma said something to Simcoe that Patrick couldn't quite catch, and the dog bounded over to Tristan, who dropped to his knees to hug the kelpie. Patrick joined Gemma at the counter.

"Is he okay?" she asked, softly.

"Yeah," he said, "and his story's consistent, although he didn't see the bear. I'm wondering if that man planted it in his mind."

"Yeah, I wondered that too," Gemma said. "I wasn't able to get license plates, and apparently our trio paid with cash. But the manager has agreed to email me a copy of the surveillance footage. They also contacted the police, but they said the earliest they can get an officer out here would be tomorrow, which makes sense considering a storm's coming."

"Not to mention that the suspect left," Patrick added, "and no one was hurt."

The waitress reappeared through the door with a chocolate brownie and a large silver bowl filled with water and asked if it would be okay if Tristan had free dessert on the house before they hit the road. There was a soft kindness in the older woman's eyes, and Patrick thanked God for the random act of kindness. Patrick thanked her and then turned to his son. "Just stay where I can see you. I want to leave in five. We've got to make sure we reach the island before the storm hits and the bridge shuts down."

Tristan looked happy and relieved that he was no longer being questioned. The waitress sat the dessert on a table and bowl of water down on the floor for Simcoe, then set the bill and some chocolates on the counter and retreated back into the kitchen. Tristan climbed onto the seat and immediately turned back to his game. Simcoe looked up at Gemma.

"Go," she said, "and stay with Tristan."

The K-9 woofed softly and walked over to him. Patrick watched the boy and dog for a moment, vaguely aware as Gemma reached across the counter for a pen and a paper napkin and started scribbling something. When he looked back, she'd written three words in all capital letters—*RUST, UMBER* and *BONE*.

"Who're they?" he whispered.

"Suspects," she said, then blushed slightly. "Or at least, my current nicknames for them. I find giving my targets names helps me to find them. Specifically, these are the designer shades of brown that the three men were wearing. Those wool fedoras and coats those men had are unbelievably expensive. We're talking eight hundred dollars for the hat and a couple thousand for the coat. Maybe they were purchased from the same place."

"So, Rust would be the man with the reddish-brown coat who fired at the potentially imaginary bear?" he asked.

"Yup," she said. "Bone had the lightest coat—"

"And white hair," Patrick supplied, "with a thin nose." She jotted the description down. "Which would make Umber the man in the darkest coat and the largest of the three."

Which was saying something as all of them had been over six feet tall and built like former linebackers.

"I also saw a woman," Gemma added. "She left when I arrived and I didn't get a good look at her, but Simcoe thought she smelled like drugs. Hopefully, she turns up on the surveillance footage. The police commissioner is planning to announce to the media tomorrow that the Noëlville Serial Killer's first victim was really Tristan's mother, Lucy."

Which didn't give Patrick much time to figure out how to break the news to his son.

"I thought they had to notify the next of kin," Patrick started to say. Then he caught himself. "Let me guess. Her parents are listed as next of kin?"

And not a man she'd never been married to and who'd never reported her missing. Even though they'd had a child together. To be honest, Patrick had never met the Marshes, who lived on the West Coast, and he hadn't thought of them in years.

"We'll want to collect those letters the fake Lucy sent and arrange a police presence outside your home. Fortunately, my whole team is scheduled to be on the island in less than forty-eight hours for Finnick's wedding." Gemma's boss was marrying a woman from Patrick's hometown on the morning of Christmas Eve. "Anything else I need to know?"

"Fake Lucy sent Christmas presents too," Patrick whispered.

"What?" Gemma's eyes widened.

"Yeah," Patrick said, and silently thanked God that he'd never told his son about them. "I opened them all. Just typical preteen boy stuff—clothes, shoes and video games. Even a teen-sized punching bag for boxing."

"What about the game console?" Gemma asked. "LMNTL is top-of-the-line and very expensive."

Huh, he'd had no idea. "No," he said, "he bought that one himself, off a friend, with his allowance."

Gemma's eyebrows rose, but she didn't question it. Tristan

had made quick work of the brownie, Simcoe was finishing her drink and the waitress was back and wiping down the tables.

"I'm going to wait here for the surveillance footage," Gemma said. "If there's anything out of the ordinary I'll call you. Otherwise, I'll give you a shout tomorrow after I talk to my team. In the meantime, if our fake Lucy reaches out again, you call us, okay?"

"Will do." He brushed his hand against Gemma's elbow. "Thank you, for everything."

"No problem," Gemma said. "Talk soon."

She tied her scarf in a knot around her neck. It was the color of robin's eggs and seemed to brighten the blue of her eyes. Her gaze was serious, but her smile was genuine and strangely beautiful, and somehow he found it hard to turn away. He turned his attention back to the counter, pocketed the mint-flavored chocolates the waitress had left on their bill and left more than enough cash to cover their meal. Then he walked over to his son and waited while Tristan gave Simcoe a final hug goodbye.

Patrick and Tristan headed out into the night. A cold wind blew against their bodies. Sleet struck the ground. When they reached the van and got in, Patrick mounted his cell phone on the dashboard, set the GPS for home and pulled out of the lot. As he drove, the lights of the diner faded in the distance and the darkness of rural Ontario surrounded him.

"I need you to promise me you won't go anywhere without telling me," Patrick said.

"Dad, I'm not a little kid," Tristan said, but his voice sounded less than certain.

"I know," Patrick said. "But that's not the point."

Lord, how am I going to ever tell my son that his mother is dead at the hands of a serial killer?

"This world is a wonderful, amazing and incredible place full of good people," Patrick went on. "But it's also a messy place with mean and dangerous people in it too. And it's not always clear which ones are which. Not even for adults like me."

Suddenly, a pair of bright lights flew out of the darkness toward them so quickly, all Patrick could do was clench the wheel, try to swerve and pray.

"Brace yourself!" Patrick shouted.

Save us, Lord!

Headlights blinded his vision. He pulled hard onto the right-hand shoulder of the highway, but it was too late. A deafening metallic crunch filled his ears as the oncoming vehicle smashed into the driver's side of the van, crushing the hood right in front of him like a concertina. The van shuttered to a stop, tossing Patrick and Tristan hard against their seat belts. "Tristan, you okay?"

"I think so." Tristan's face was pale in the glow of the van's interior light. "Why did they hit us?"

"I don't know." But even as Patrick could feel a breath of relief filling his chest, he looked to see two silhouettes stepping toward them out of the glaring lights.

It was two men in fedoras and long wool coats, and both of them were holding guns.

"Get in the back!" Patrick ordered. "Now."

"But Dad—"

"Don't argue, just do it."

God, please be our Shield and our Protector.

Tristan unbuckled his seatbelt and squeezed between the gap in the seats and into the back of the van.

"Get out of the van!" Umber bellowed. "Hands up!"

Patrick's heart beat like a drum in his chest. Patrick prayed the men hadn't seen his son. If it was one man with a gun, Patrick would've tried to jump him and disarm him, but with two, the risk was too high that one would start shooting and Tristan could get hit.

Now all he could do was distract them long enough for Tristan to get to safety.

Bone strode toward the driver's side door. Umber stood behind him, providing cover. He didn't see Rust anywhere or the men's second vehicle.

"Tristan, when I open my door I need you to jump out the back and run!" Patrick said. "Whatever happens, don't stop. Get back to the diner! Find Gemma! Get help!"

"Dad, I—"

"It'll be okay. Just go!"

"Get out of the van now!" Bone ordered. "You're coming with us!"

Patrick reached around and grabbed a flare out of the back of the van. Not much of a weapon against two guns, but not bad for a distraction. Patrick lit the flare, then threw the driver's side door open as flames seemed to erupt from the cone in his hand. He heard the back door open and his son's feet hit the ground.

"I'm here!" Patrick shouted. "What do you want?"

And for a moment, it seemed to keep the men back, as he waved the flames in front of him like an animal trainer keeping the beasts at bay. But all too soon, it began to flicker and die.

Then came a sound like a shotgun blast. Something hard smacked like a rock against his skull. He dropped the flare and fell to his knees, as the world went black.

TWO

"I have an unbelievably bad feeling about this," Gemma admitted to Caleb. "Something bad is going on involving this dad and his kid, and I don't know what it is."

She was sitting in her car in the diner parking lot, with Simcoe curled up in the front seat and her colleague—Corporal Caleb Pine—on speakerphone.

"But you don't see anything suspicious on the security camera footage?" he asked.

"No," she admitted. She'd watched the footage on her phone as soon as the email came in but hadn't seen anything. That didn't stop her gut from insisting something was wrong. "I'm sending it to you to now. Take a quick look at it and tell me what you think."

The Send icon on her screen seemed to spin endlessly before it sent.

"I got it," he said. There was a creak, which she knew meant her colleague had leaned back in his chair. She replayed the same black-and-white video, which she knew he was watching now. It showed the back of the diner, with a smattering of overturned crates and a whole lot of trees lying beyond. She saw Tristan coming around the corner. His face turned away from the camera, but he didn't spend that much time looking down at his computer game. Instead, he just stood there awkwardly.

"What's he doing?" Caleb asked.

"Nothing," Gemma admitted.

"Since when do kids leave a building in wet and freezing cold weather to do nothing?"

She glanced at Simcoe. The kelpie's large ears twitched to show she was listening, but the dog's eyes didn't open. Gemma turned back to the video.

It didn't have audio, but she could tell from the way Tristan leaped that something in the woods had indeed startled him. A faction of a second later, Rust rushed into view and fired into the trees.

"He definitely didn't aim at the kid," Caleb said.

"No, he didn't," Gemma admitted.

They continued to watch as Rust turned to Tristan and said something. Presumably reinforcing the story about the bear.

"It's just so rare to see a bear in December," she added. "A wolf or a deer I'd have believed."

But wolves tended to avoid people and she couldn't imagine why the man would've shot at a deer.

Seconds later, they saw Simcoe charge around the corner and leap on Rust. Looked like the dog had caught him by surprise. They kept watching in silence as Patrick and Gemma arrived and confronted Rust. Then he left, they left, and the feed went back to showing trees.

"There's nothing else on the tape after this," she said.

Caleb exhaled a noisy breath.

"Two minutes and fifty-four seconds," he said. "That's how long Tristan was alone and out back doing nothing. What if he wasn't alone? What if there was someone else there, just out of frame?"

"And then our suspect shot at them?"

"Maybe," Caleb said. "I don't know."

But he raised an interesting question. This was why she'd wanted a second opinion from a colleague. Especially one like Caleb, whom she could always count on to be blunt and unsparing in his opinions.

Truth was she'd never found it easy to ask for help. In fact, during her first major private eye investigation, her own brother had assumed she was dead, because of how determined she'd been not to tell him what was really going on. But she liked to think she'd changed since then. Now, she was part of a team.

"Do you think the kid is lying?" she asked. "His dad believes him."

"Everybody lies," Caleb said, "Not always on purpose. Some people lie to themselves, even when they think they're telling the truth. That's why I never had kids."

Nah, Gemma thought, the real reason Caleb had never had kids was he'd had his heart broken badly by someone in the past and never gotten over it. But she didn't know the story there, and Finnick had strictly forbidden her from digging into any of her colleagues' histories.

"I'll head to the island tomorrow, meet up with Patrick and collect everything he can give me on this fake mom business," Caleb said. "I agree, the whole thing is beyond sus—"

A sudden clang jolted Gemma as two palms slammed hard against the passenger side of her car.

She spun. It was Tristan. His face was so pale it was almost gray.

"They kidnapped my dad!" he shouted.

What was he talking about? She practically flung herself across the seat in a rush to open the door for him. Simcoe leaped up and scrambled onto Tristan's lap as the boy climbed inside her car and onto the passenger seat.

"What happened?" Worry flooded her heart. "Who took your dad?"

"They... He... The men in hats..." Tristan wrapped both arms around the kelpie. Simcoe nestled her head into his neck. Tristan was shivering and shaking so hard that he could barely speak. "We need to call the police."

"It's okay, kid." Caleb's voice filled the car. It was both warmer and more reassuring than she'd ever heard it before. "My name is Caleb. I'm a police officer and I'm here to help. Just tell Gemma what happened and I'll make sure law enforcement are on it."

Tristan's eyes darted around in panic. The kid looked ready to pass out, and she wasn't sure if it was from the added shock of hearing Caleb's disembodied voice or that the adrenaline that had propelled him here was starting to wear off.

Lord, I don't know what's going on, and I'm terrified for Patrick. Please help calm Tristan down and get the help we need.

"Hey, it's okay," Gemma said. "You're safe now and we're going to help your dad. Just tell us what happened."

Tristan gulped a painful-sounding breath, then haltingly began to explain how he'd been in the van with Patrick when suddenly a car had intentionally crashed into them. He'd seen two men with guns, and his dad had told him to run.

"They said we had to go with them." His voice shook. "There were gunshots. I just kept running and didn't look back." A sob choked in the youth's throat. He ran his hand over the kelpie's head, and Simcoe licked his fingers.

"I've alerted Ontario Provincial Police," Caleb said, soberly, "and reported it as a kidnapping." She assumed he'd put her call on mute and called it in on a separate line. "They're dispatching officers and on the lookout for the vehicle."

What he was leaving out was the fact that the closest OPP

division was ninety minutes away, and there was no way helicopters would be dispatched in this weather.

"But we're going to go rescue him now, right?" Tristan asked.

Lord, help me help this child...

"Gemma isn't a police officer," Caleb answered before she found her words. "She doesn't have a gun or a badge or anything like that. But what she can do is take you somewhere safe—"

"No!" Tristan cut him off. "We have to go help my dad now before it's too late!"

He reached out and grabbed Gemma's arm. She turned to face him. Hope and fear pooled in his hazel eyes. He looked so much like his father.

"I know where the van crashed," Tristan said. "It's not that far away. Once they get him in their car they can take him anywhere, and the police might never find him."

The kid was right.

"Gemma," Caleb said, firmly. "You're not a cop. There's nothing you can do—"

"There's plenty I can do," Gemma pointed out. "I can take pictures of the crash scene before the snow destroys them. I can look for clues. I can give GPS coordinates to the OPP—"

"And what if the armed men are still there?" Caleb said. "What if they kidnap you too? You can't just go chasing after a group of armed men with a little kid—"

"I'm not a little kid!" Tristan's voice rose. "And he's my dad!"

Help me, Lord! I can't just sit here and do nothing.

"I know we might not be able to save him." A sob hitched in Tristan's voice. "But we're the only hope he's got."

"He's right," Gemma said. She felt her jaw set with determination. Time was ticking. If she had any hope of saving

Patrick, she had to go now. "Simcoe, get in the back and lay down. Tristan, put on your seat belt. Caleb, I'm going with Tristan to the crash scene," she said. "You know I've got a task force GPS tracker on my car. You can use it to keep track of my location and give the police more accurate data on Patrick's accident."

"You can't do this!" Caleb said.

"I can't not do it either," she said, "and you'd do the same if you were in my shoes."

She waited as Simcoe settled herself in the back and Tristan's seat belt clicked.

"At least promise me you'll keep a safe distance," Caleb called, "and that you won't do anything stupid!"

"I promise," she said. Or at least, she'd do her very best. "I'm muting you now, Caleb, just so I can focus on the road. The weather is getting bad, and I can't have you arguing in my ear."

She muted him before he could answer.

Then she peeled out of the lot and into the darkness.

Patrick woke up to find himself being dragged slowly down a slope and across muddy ground. Gloved hands gripped him by the arms. The sleet had hardened into pellets of ice that now smacked his skin, but at least they were waking him up. His head throbbed like he'd just been stung in the same spot by a thousand bees, and it hurt so much when he tried to open his eyes, he immediately closed them again. Probably better to let his captors think he was still unconscious anyway. If he had to guess, he'd been hit with a rubber bullet or maybe a beanbag round. Not fatal but definitely not pleasant. He had no idea how long he'd been out for, who these two men were or where they were taking him. But as he felt himself slowly return to consciousness, only one thought burned like a flame at the front of his mind.

Tristan!

Had his son escaped? Had he found help?

But even as he began to pray for Tristan's survival, Patrick felt his body jolt as the two men dropped him. Then he heard their voices rise in anger. Snippets of conversation moved in and out through the recesses of his pain-filled head, and Patrick did his best to patch them together into coherent thoughts.

The car wouldn't start... The road had been icy, and the accident had been more severe than expected... They had to get Patrick away from the road while they waited for someone to come with a different car, but they didn't quite seem sure what to do with him after that...

And most importantly, they'd let Tristan escape.

"Where is he?" Umber bellowed.

"I don't know!" Bone shouted back. "Kid ran really fast! And it's dark out here!"

Thank You, God! His son had escaped. *Please keep him safe. Guide him to someone who can help him, and show me what to do.* Suddenly, Gemma's heart-shaped face filled his mind with her beautiful blue eyes and dark wisps of hair brushing her cheeks. Had he unwittingly put her life in danger too by meeting with her? *Lord, please protect her.*

He was at the mercy of an inexplicable and undefinable danger that was all too real and violent, nonetheless. Lucy—the only woman he'd ever offered his heart to—was dead at the hands of a serial killer. In a cruel twist, the fact somebody had been reaching out to him posing as her made knowing that she was gone even worse. He'd once loved her deeply, and he'd never moved past her betrayal and opened his heart to somebody new. Hadn't been on a date in over a decade, let alone held another woman in his arms. It wasn't because he'd missed Lucy or the way her harsh and mocking words seemed to tear him into strips, leaving his self-esteem in tatters. He'd thought that he'd loved her, and he'd mistaken the fact that she kept coming back whenever she hit rock bottom to mean she must've loved him too, despite the fact she'd kept refusing his marriage proposals, had never wanted Tristan and would disappear for days and nights with strangers.

No, Patrick hadn't missed her, so much as felt completely broken by his failure to convince her that he and Tristan were worth caring about.

"We don't need the kid!" Bone's voice rose again.

"The kid is leverage!" Umber shot back. "You think we don't need leverage?"

The question was loud, angry and sarcastic. Patrick could tell by the way the other man swore under his breath in response that he was moments away from giving in and going to look for Tristan. Time to draw the attention back to himself.

God, give me speed...

Patrick scrambled to his feet and ran, pelting through the darkness in the opposite direction of the diner. The sudden burst of swearing and the rush of footsteps coming toward him let him know he'd managed to catch them by surprise.

Angry voices yelled for him to stop. A gunshot fired somewhere behind him in the darkness, and he felt an all too real bullet pass by his ear. Miss. Another shot. This one hit him in the left shoulder and knocked him forward a step with the pressure of a ten-pound fist. He stumbled, nearly fell and silently thanked God when nothing broke or snapped. Patrick kept running, pushing through the icy branches and tripping over rocks in the darkness. Then came the full body blow of someone barreling into his legs and tackling him from behind. He pitched forward and landed on his knees, then before he could find his footing again he felt somebody press the barrel of a gun to the back of his head.

Was this one loaded with bullets or beanbag rounds? He couldn't tell. But at this range, either could be fatal.

"Hands up!"

Patrick knelt and raised his hands until they were level with his ears. Bone stepped around in front of him, training his pistol on him. Guess that meant the man now pressing a gun into the back of his head was Umber.

"Who are you?" Bone demanded.

Patrick was so startled by the funny question that he'd have laughed if the situation wasn't so deadly serious. They didn't know who he was? Then why had they smashed into his vehicle? Why had they tried to kidnap him and considered hunting his son?

Why was one of them holding a gun to his head now?

"I'm Patrick Craft. My name is on the side of the van…"

Umber walked around in front of him, dragging the muzzle of the gun along Patrick's head. Then he stopped in front of him and took a step back. Okay, so there were still two guns trained on him, but now they were both at least a foot away from his head. A small improvement to his situation, but one he silently thanked God for.

Umber's eyes narrowed and his words were slow and deliberate.

"Were. Is. The. Stash?"

"What stash?" Patrick blinked. He'd guessed this was about a serial killer and his ex-wife. Now there was some kind of theft involved? "I don't know what you're looking for or what any of this is about."

But it seemed the men weren't about to listen. Umber's gloved hand flew across Patrick's face with a stinging blow.

"Tell us where the stash is!" The criminal's voice rose. "Or we'll kill you, and then we'll kill that woman and your son."

THREE

Gemma's eyes locked on the dark road ahead. The sleet had turned to ice, and the road was growing slick beneath her tires. She pressed her foot against the accelerator, urging her small blue hatchback to speed as fast as she dared, easing up only when she felt her traction begin to slide. Patrick's warm but reluctant smile filled her mind. He cared so deeply about his son. He'd been worried for Tristan's safety—and now it looked like maybe they hadn't taken the danger seriously enough. Tristan's face was turned toward the window as he stared out at the darkness. She glanced quickly to the rearview mirror and saw Simcoe sitting tall and alert in the back seat, as if the K-9 was on the lookout for danger. Gemma gritted her teeth and prayed.

Lord, I don't know who our enemy is, I don't know what I'm up against, and I don't have any idea what I'm going to be able to do to help. Caleb's right, I'm not a cop and I need to keep Tristan safe. I just don't want to give up on saving Patrick if there's something I can do. Please, guide me. Show me when to act and when I need to run.

Terrifying memories began to prick at the back of her mind—ones she'd tried hard to forget. It had been about a year and a half since a killer she'd been investigating had run her off this very road, into the river, and fired his gun at her again and again as her car had sunk into the watery depths. She'd nearly drowned. A sharp pain began to spread in her chest, like her rib cage was tightening around her lungs until it hurt to breathe. She'd never told anyone—even her brother—about how the memories of that night still filled her with an overwhelming panic, until she felt almost like she was drowning inside.

Did Finnick suspect? Was that why he'd let her take Simcoe?

Gemma forced the memories away, firmly pushing them to the back of her mind. That was then and this was now. Back then she'd been trying to investigate a serial killer all on her own. As a PI, she'd frequently looked into cold cases, searching for new information to see if she could play a part in closing any of them. Now, she was part of a close-knit team with plenty of resources, who had her back if things went downhill. They were able to track each other's cars via GPS, not to mention Jackson had loaded her car with an extensively well-stocked emergency kit along with enough flashing lights, flares and even loud speakers so she'd always be able to signal for help if she was ever in trouble.

When the cold case unit had been formed back in November of last year, it was comprised of Finnick and his K-9, Nippy, Gemma's brother, Jackson, and his K-9, Hudson, along with Caleb and Gemma. A few weeks later, Lucas Harper and his K-9 partner, Michigan, joined the team. But Finnick was currently taking time off for his wedding and relocating his family to Toronto. Jackson was with his wife, Amy, and their daughter, Skye, celebrating an exhibition of Amy's paintings at a Christmas art show in Aurora. Amy was Gemma's best friend, and she was so proud of her. Now the team also included Sergeant Blake Murphy of the Ontario Provincial Police, who was acting as their liaison with the provincial police's investigation into the Noëlville Serial Killer, along with another cop named Oscar—a mystery detective with no last name, no history and no police file she could dig into. He'd apparently been deep undercover for years, but Finnick trusted him implicitly. She was grateful for her team and knew she could count on them if she needed help.

"I think we're almost there," Tristan said. His voice was so hopeful and optimistic, but she could hear the tremor of fear hiding underneath. Silently she prayed that she wouldn't let him down.

Suddenly, her phone began to chime with a series of texts coming in fast and furious from Jackson. She knew, without even having to check them, that Caleb had alerted her brother to what she was trying to do and part of her almost wished he hadn't. Jackson was too far away to help. All he could do was worry, which would just add to her stress.

Then again, there was no one on the planet she trusted more than Jackson. Not to mention she'd promised to never disappear on him in a moment of crisis ever again. Her eyes darted to the screen.

Caleb told me what you're doing!

You gotta stop.

I get it. You have a good heart and you're really brave. But you're not a cop.

Gemma, please! I don't want to lose you again!

"Who's that?" Tristan asked, "and what does he mean by losing you again?"

She glanced at him. "Once when I was working on a case

a really bad guy came after me and tried to kill me," she told the kid honestly. "My brother, Jackson, thought I was dead."

Because she'd been so shaken and so stubborn she'd let him believe that instead of going to him for help like she should've.

Tristan's brows rose in surprise. "Did you get the guy?"

"Yes," she said. "With the help of my team. Everything turned out fine. But since then we've promised to always check in with each other, just to make sure we both know we're okay."

"There it is!" Tristan's voice rose.

She looked to where he was pointing. Then, through the haze of hail pebbles, she saw the outline of two vehicles on the side of the road ahead.

Gemma pulled onto the shoulder, as close to the tree line as she dared, cut the lights and peered into the darkness. It looked like one of the two expensive cars she'd seen in the diner parking lot had smashed headfirst into Patrick's construction van. The car was completely totaled, and the van wasn't much better.

Her hand rose to her mouth.

Lord, have mercy on us all...

Her eyes searched the darkness. There was no one in sight.

"I'm going to get out of the car now and walk over there to see if I can find out what's going on," she said. "I need you to stay in the car."

She barely got the words out before Tristan began to shake his head. "No, no, I'm coming too."

Lord, help me get through to him and help him to listen. I can't risk getting out of the car if there's any possibility he's going to come running after me.

"No, Tristan. I need you to stay on the line with me." Caleb's voice filled the car again. It was only then she'd remembered their phones had been set up with an emergency mute override. He must've unmuted himself at some point.

Thank You, Lord, for Caleb.

"I need your help, Tristan," Caleb went on firmly. "You're my lookout. It's your job to honk the horn and warn Gemma if you see danger coming, and I'm counting on you to tell me everything that's happening, so that we can keep Gemma safe and find your dad. Can you do that for me?"

She held her breath but needn't have worried.

"All right, Officer," Tristan said. He sat up straight, and his voice sounded a little older than it had moments earlier. "I'll keep watch and report."

Gemma opened her mouth to thank Caleb, only to feel a lump form in her throat at the palpable relief she could hear in Caleb's voice as he said, "Sounds good. Thank you."

She glanced back to her K-9. Simcoe's intelligent face was focused on her, as if waiting for orders, and she found herself wishing she had two dogs—one to guard Tristan and one to help guide her to Patrick.

"Tristan, are you okay staying in the car alone with just Caleb for a moment?" she asked. "I might need Simcoe's help to find your dad. But, as soon as I can I'll bring Simcoe right back to join you, okay?"

Tristan nodded, bravely. "Okay, if it'll help find my dad."

Gemma swallowed hard. "I'll be right back, I promise. Stay safe and listen to Caleb."

She got out of the car and signaled to Simcoe. The dog leaped through the front seat and came out the driver's side door. She closed the door, locked it behind her then cautiously made her way toward the crashed vehicle, with Simcoe by her side. Both vehicles were empty. Patrick and the men who'd run him off the road were gone. Wind and snow had erased any trace of footprints.

Help me, Lord. What do I do? How do I find Patrick?

A flash of red caught her eye inside Patrick's construction van. There was a baseball cap wedged between the driver's seat and the center console. She pulled it out. It was faded and red with the Canadian flag. The fabric was soft to the touch.

I hope this works...

She held the hat under Simcoe's nose.

"Simcoe, search," she said. "Find Patrick."

The kelpie sniffed the hat, then her head rose and she barked sharply.

"Shh," Gemma whispered, closing her fingers and thumb in the gesture Finnick had shown her. "We need to be really quiet."

Simcoe woofed again, so quietly it was like the dog was whispering too. The dog started sniffing the ground. For a moment Simcoe weaved her way around the two crashed vehicles. Then she led Gemma down the road, staying close to the tree line. Gemma pulled her hood on tight over her head and followed. For a moment, she saw nothing but a wall of trees. Then she heard the sound of shouting, rising and falling on the wind. There were two male voices. They sounded angry and demanding, but she couldn't make out the words they were saying. She signaled Simcoe back to her side, then together they crept across the slippery ground toward the shouting.

A moment later and the scene came into view at the bottom of a long and steep slope, illuminated by a cell phone light. At first she only saw Bone and Umber standing with their backs to her.

Then she saw Patrick.

He was kneeling on the ground, with his hands on his head and his chin risen high in defiance to the two men now threatening him. An unfamiliar emotion—something hot and protective—moved like a fire through her. Patrick had no badge and no gun. He was completely outnumbered. Most people in his circumstances would already be down for the count. But not Patrick. Instead, as he faced his captors, a calm and strong courage seemed to move through his form, and she knew she'd never seen anything braver in her life.

I have to rescue him! But how?

"Where's the stash?" Umber shouted.

"I don't know!" Patrick replied, "I have no idea what you're talking about!"

Patrick didn't know how long he'd been kneeling there on the ground, caught in an endless loop of answering the same question over and over again. He still had no idea who these men were, why they'd targeted him or where the third member of their crew was now. Moments earlier, he thought he'd heard the sound of an approaching car and even seen a flicker of headlights through the distant trees. But it had disappeared just as quickly as it had arrived, and the other men didn't seem to have noticed it.

Patrick wondered if he was going to die here.

Lord, please keep Tristan and Gemma safe.

Bone stepped forward and jabbed his gun in between Patrick's eyes. "I'm gonna give you to the count of five to tell me where we can find what we're looking for. Otherwise, I'm just going to pull the trigger and go looking for your woman and kid."

He couldn't tell them. He didn't know.

Lord, please save my life...

"Five," Bone shouted. "Four..."

Patrick braced his legs and prepared himself to spring, knowing he'd rather get shot on his feet fighting for the gun, then take a bullet down on his knees.

Suddenly, he heard a car on the road above, and the world

behind his kidnappers erupted in a flurry of lights and sirens. Were they police cars, firetrucks, ambulances or some combination of all three? He couldn't tell, in the absolute chaos of the flashing and spinning white, blue, red and yellow lights, and the multiple sirens blaring in overlapping whoops and shrieks. And through it all, one noise rose both clear and strong—the determined and fierce sound of a dog barking.

Bone and Umber jolted and turned toward the chaos. And somehow Patrick knew in his gut that both men would rather shoot him dead in the snow before they'd give police the opportunity to run down the hill and rescue him. He had to get out of here. Now.

As the guns moved away from Patrick's face, he struck. Leaping to his feet, he barreled into Bone, knocking the gun from his hand and sending it flying. Then he leveled a firm blow to Bone's jaw to discourage him from trying anything stupid. Bone swore, but for now he was staying down. Patrick turned to run when he felt Umber leap on his back and try to choke him from behind. He collapsed back to his knees under the weight of the bigger man. Umber's arm tightened around Patrick's neck.

"This is Corporal Caleb Pine of the Ontario Cold Case Task Force!" The police officer's voice boomed over the chaos through some loudspeaker he couldn't see. "Get your hands up and drop your weapons now!"

Thank You, Lord!

Patrick raised his elbow high and swung back, catching Umber in the jaw. The bigger man grunted and let go. Patrick ran toward the sirens without looking back. Lights blinded his eyes.

His hands rose. "My name is Patrick Craft!"

"Patrick!" Two soft but firm hands grabbed ahold of him and pulled him up the slope. He felt a dog pressing its body protectively against his legs. "It's me, Gemma! Come on, we've got to go!"

Gemma?

She grabbed his right hand and practically dragged him up the hill. Relief and confusion battled in his chest. He'd expected she'd have called the police. But not that she'd be leading the charge down the hill. "What are you doing here?"

"Rescuing you."

He could barely hear her voice above the sirens and Officer Caleb's orders that Umber and Bone must surrender.

Gemma led him up an embankment and onto the road. "Come on, we don't have much time before they realize we've tricked them."

"What?"

His vision cleared, and he finally saw what lay beyond the lights. There were no cop cars. No law enforcement at all. Just Gemma's blue hatchback, with three different siren lights plopped on the top and multiple speakers propped up in the open windows...

By his son.

"Dad!" Tristan shouted and waved from the passenger seat. A huge grin beamed across his face. "You're okay!"

"Hey, son," Patrick felt a lump form in his chest. *I didn't know if I'd ever see you again.* He dropped Gemma's hand and ran toward his boy.

And just like that Patrick could feel the fear that had begun dissipating inside him roar back to life again. Where was Corporal Pine? He could only see Gemma, a K-9 dog and his preteen son. They were still outgunned and in danger.

He leaped into the passenger seat and buckled up, just as Tristan scrambled through the seats into the back. "Let's get out of here," he urged.

Gemma ran around to the driver's seat.

"Simcoe, get into your seat," she called, as she climbed in. Patrick watched as the dog got into the center seat next to his son and sat tall. Tristan buckled the dog's harness as Gemma instructed, then did his own seat belt.

Patrick could hear Umber and Bone shouting in anger from the woods.

"Do the hostiles have working vehicles?" Caleb's voice asked. He was on speakerphone—he wasn't there at all. Tristan had dismantled the other speaker system he'd been holding, but they'd realize Gemma's diversion soon enough. They had no real backup. They needed to move.

"No, not yet," Patrick said. "But I don't suggest we stick around until they get one."

A pair of bright headlights loomed behind them in the darkness.

Was it Rust, come to get Umber and Bone?

"We've got to get out of here!" Patrick shouted. "Now!"

He glanced at Gemma, expecting to see her throw the car into Drive and hit the gas. Instead, she sat there, frozen, with her hands gripping the wheel and her eyes locked on the darkness ahead. The headlights loomed closer. He could now see the shapes of Umber and Bone emerging from the darkness to his right. "Come on! We've got to go!"

But Gemma still seemed locked in place.

What was wrong with her?

Instinctively, Patrick reached across the front seat, grabbed a hold of Gemma's right hand and squeezed it tightly. *Lord, help her. Help us...* "Are you okay?"

Gemma blinked, he pulled his hand back, and then she gunned the engine and the small car shot down the road, just as smoothly as if she'd never hesitated. She cut the flashing lights and sirens. He looked back. The headlights behind them were growing smaller by the second, which meant the vehicle must've stopped. Had they stopped by the crash to see if anyone needed help? Or were they there to collect the men who'd just attacked them?

Moments later the headlights he'd seen behind them had disappeared entirely and darkness filled his gaze again. As if on cue, the predicted snow finally hit, in thick heavy flurries that swallowed up the car in a cloud of white.

"Storm's arrived a lot sooner than expected, Caleb," Gemma said, "and it's hitting with a vengeance." Windshield wipers sped back and forth, ineffectually shoving the flakes around. "You still got us on GPS?"

"Yeah, but it's patchy." Caleb sounded concerned. "Your location keeps jumping around on me. Also, you're right about the storm. It hit faster and fiercer than anyone forecast."

There were no streetlights this deep in rural Ontario and very few street signs, if it had even been possible to see one. The storm was growing so quickly, Patrick could barely see anything outside the window now but inky black darkness punctuated by white specks hurling themselves at the windows. He could hardly even see the trees.

"Can you direct us to Manitoulin Island?" he asked Caleb. "We can get police to meet us at the house."

"Sorry, no can do," Caleb said. "They're already in the process of shutting down the swing bridge overnight thanks to the sudden shift from ice to snow. I'm afraid you're grounded on the mainland until morning."

"What if we find the closest city with a motel?" Gemma asked.

"Unfortunately, the storm has brought down power lines all across Ontario," Caleb said. The sound of typing came down the phone. "Looks like we're dealing with cascading power failures. I don't know how much longer you're even going to have cell service. I'm surprised we've still got an open line to each other."

Gemma nodded slowly to herself, then her lips set in a grim line.

"So, we make our way to my cottage on Cedar Lake," she said. "Thirty minutes from here. We'll hunker down there overnight. Then we'll meet there as a team in the morning as soon as the roads are cleared. All available hands on deck."

"Sounds like the best possible solution to me," Caleb said. "I'll let everyone know and keep the lines of communication open with you as long as possible. Hopefully, we'll be able to get to you by ten thirty or eleven."

"Bring bread and eggs," Gemma said. "I'll make French toast for everyone. Thankfully I'm well stocked on coffee and maple syrup."

There was a forced cheerfulness in her voice, like she was determined to stay positive whatever happened.

"That plan good by you, Patrick?" she asked, without taking her eyes off the road.

"Not ideal," he admitted. He'd hoped to get Tristan home tonight, before the bridge closed. "But it's the best we've got."

While Gemma drove, Caleb interviewed Patrick over speakerphone about Umber, Bone and Rust, getting down everything he could remember in order to file a police report. Patrick relayed everything that happened since he left the diner.

"My sister-in-law, Amy, is really good at cold sketching people's faces," Gemma added. "We'll get her to do composite sketches of Umber, Rust and Bone from our memories, which we can run against available criminal databases and also get out to law enforcement and the media."

Her eyes met his for a fraction of a second before snapping back to the road. But even in that brief flicker of a glance he could feel the warmth of reassurance and faith in her gaze.

FOUR

It took them over half an hour to reach Gemma's cabin. For the first twenty minutes or so, Caleb remained on the line and was able to help guide them along the best back roads. Then the phone line finally died and a tense silence filled the vehicle, punctuated only by the sound of the windshield wipers squeaking and wind buffeting hard against the car.

Gemma's hands were clenched so tightly on the steering wheel, Patrick wondered if her fingers ached. Worry lines creased her beautiful face. She looked frightened and focused, as if she was fighting an internal battle that no one else could see. The memory of how she'd frozen when they'd first leaped in the car prickled at the back of his mind, like a component that didn't quite fit right in its socket, but he didn't want to risk throwing her off by asking her about it now. There was a lot they needed to talk about. Back in the diner, they'd barely scratched the surface of the much longer conversation they needed to have about what had happened to Lucy, and his mind had been left whirling. Lucy was dead. She'd been murdered by a serial killer. Someone had been impersonating her.

But why? And why now?

Patrick glanced over his shoulder at his son sitting in the back seat. For a while, his son had been playing with his gaming device, and Patrick couldn't tell if Tristan had been using the game to distract himself from the terrible things that had happened that night, or if the fact he'd plugged into the game so quickly meant the crash and the gunmen hadn't really impacted him much at all. Then again, it was also possible that his son just felt numb and the full impact of everything would hit him later. Now the game's battery had died along with cell signal, and his son was staring out the window with a blank look, watching the blur of gray, black and white go by.

"All good, bud?" Patrick asked.

Tristan gave Patrick a thumbs-up, and Patrick gave him one back.

"We can talk if you want," Patrick offered.

But his son turned back to the window, and Patrick looked forward again.

Lord, how am I going to tell Tristan his mother is dead at the hands of a serial killer?

He'd lost track of times he'd prayed that same prayer since learning that Lucy was dead, and now, he felt no closer to an answer. Especially after everything that had happened with Umber, Bone and Rust. The supposed run-in with the bear behind the diner was looking more suspicious by the moment. Had Rust been trying to kidnap Tristan? If so, why had he fired into the woods? Had someone else been there? His heart felt heavy with words he couldn't say and questions he couldn't ask. At least, not for now.

Finally, the vehicle slowed, and he looked up to see a yellow light glimmering ahead of them through the storm. Gemma pulled to a stop, the four of them got out, and Patrick got his first glimpse of the cabin.

It was two stories tall, with a slanted overhang that jutted out from underneath the second-story windows and created a pocket of shelter on the back porch for them to huddle under as Gemma unlocked the door.

Thick fir trees surrounded them on all sides, but somewhere beyond the snow and darkness he could hear the faint and chilly sound of water lashing against ice as it was whipped up by the storm. Dazzling golden lights decorated a handful of trees closest to the cottage.

They stepped inside, and immediately the scent of pine wood, acrylic paint and family baking filled his senses. He shrugged off his coat and pulled off his boots, letting the lingering warmth left in the building begin to thaw his limbs.

The square-shaped cottage had an open-concept main floor, with huge floor to ceiling windows that stretched two-stories high, all the way up to the roof. He expected that during daylight hours they looked out over the lake. The Christmas tree beside the fireplace was almost as tall as the room itself. It was decorated with hundreds of colored balls, along with an array of handmade farm animals, angels, teddy bears and toy soldiers.

A metal spiral staircase stood opposite the windows and led up to the wooden landing of a smaller second floor. Judging by the numbers of doors, he guessed there were two bedrooms, both of which looked out over the driveway.

At one end of the main floor was a small kitchenette, and at the other sat an easel surrounded by art supplies.

Gemma took off Simcoe's K-9 vest.

"Okay," she said to the dog. "You're off the clock."

Simcoe woofed and made a beeline for a soft shag carpet on the floor and rolled around on her back, with her three paws waving in the air.

"This place is amazing!" Tristan charged into the main room without pausing to shed his winter gear. "Do you have a lake? Is there a boat?"

"Yes and yes," Gemma replied, "but the lake's in that in-between stage where it's frozen around the edges and still thawed in the middle."

Which would line up with the sound of water that Patrick heard. Gemma moved to the kitchen and began opening doors and getting out mugs.

"Cool!" Tristan's eyes darted around the room. "Is there somewhere I can plug in my gaming console?"

"There's a power bar in the first bedroom upstairs," Gemma said. "But would you guys mind building a fire while I make us some hot apple cider first?"

"And take off your boots, son!" Patrick called. "Miss Locke doesn't want you tracking muddy footprints through her house."

"You can call me Gemma," she told Tristan, with a soft smile as he did a U-turn and dashed back to the entrance, to hang his coat on the rack next to Patrick's and deposit his boots by the door.

Patrick made a mental note to talk to his son about limiting his screen time. He had no idea just how addicted to his gaming device Tristan had become. But for now, considering everything else that was going on, he'd let it slide.

Patrick joined his son at the well-stocked pile of wood behind the fireplace, and for a long moment, he enjoyed the brief break from the worry and chaos, as together they built a fire, stacking the larger pieces of wood, tucking smaller branches underneath and finally adding paper for kindling.

A momentary bubble of peace surrounded them as he and Tristan watched the flames flicker and take hold, and the gentle scent of hot apples and cinnamon filled the air. Gemma brought three mugs of hot cider to the coffee table along with a small plate of gingerbread cookies and cinnamon sticks. Simcoe stretched out in front of the fire approvingly, closed her eyes and began to snore. Tristan took two cookies and a mug and scampered upstairs, then closed the bedroom door behind him. Gemma sat down in a comfortable-looking green chair, and Patrick sat down on the couch. A heavy silence fell between them, as if they were both mentally gathering up the words they needed to say.

"This place is incredible," Patrick said.

"Thanks," Gemma said. "I used to live here and run the bookstore in town, before I landed my job in the city with the Cold Case Task Force. Now, Jackson and Amy live here with their baby, Skye, but it's tricky with Jackson's work on the task force."

"I can't imagine anyone wanting to live in the city when they could live out here," Patrick admitted.

"And I can't imagine ever giving up the access to solve crimes that being in the city gives me," Gemma said, with a mild smile. "Honestly, Jackson's attempts to work remotely have been a dismal failure. I mean, we don't even have internet access right now, and you live on an island where everyone gets stuck whenever the weather gets bad enough."

She stirred her apple cider with the cinnamon stick.

"There are two beds in the room that Tristan's in right now," Gemma added, "if you and Tristan want to share one room and I'll take the other."

"If it's all the same to you I'd rather sleep down here on the couch and keep watch."

"Sounds good," Gemma said. "It folds out. Although, Simcoe will probably try to join you at some point in the night."

She looked at the dog sleeping by the fireplace.

"How long have you had her?" Patrick asked.

"Only a few weeks," Gemma said. "I still don't know if I'm providing her a temporary home or a permanent one. All depends on whether she's retired from K-9 service or goes back to official K-9 work." She sighed, and he watched as shadows cast from the flickering flames danced across the beautiful lines of her face. "Simcoe is probably going to be retired for not being able to pass the recertification course due to how she was injured on the job, which is a shame because she's an incredibly talented dog and only two years old."

"What happened to her human partner?" Patrick asked.

"He was fired," Gemma said, bluntly. "He was already on probation for making quite a few mistakes on the job. Abandoning Simcoe and the children he been tasked with rescuing once the house caught fire was the final straw. Thankfully, they all made it out okay. She's an incredibly brave dog."

"I'll say." Patrick blew out a hard breath and turned to Simcoe. "I'm so sorry that happened to you. You're better off without him."

"I imagine that as volunteer fire chief you've run into more than your fair share of burning buildings," Gemma said.

"Yeah... I've lost of how many." Patrick chuckled. "I've also rescued a lot of people from ice storms and frozen vehicles at the side of the road, too. Not to mention every imaginable kind of water rescue on Lake Huron and Georgian Bay."

"In other words, the right guy to have around in a crisis." Gemma smiled. "So, you're a Small Town Jack of All Rescue Trades?"

Heat rose to the back of his neck. Maybe it was just warmth from the fire. "I wouldn't go that far."

The faint sounds of electronic cars revving their engines and explosions popping trickled down from above them. Patrick glanced up at the closed bedroom door and wondered if Gemma had suggested that Tristan plug his game in upstairs in order to give them some privacy.

"My son might be a bit too addicted to his game," Patrick said. "Looks like I should maybe start talking to him about spending so much time on gaming. You said those things are expensive?"

"Very," Gemma said. "Probably the top children's toy company in the country. You know the latest LMNTL console has chatting capability. Do you let him use it to talk to anyone online?"

"No," Patrick said. "He knows he's not allowed."

"Well, he seems like a wonderful kid," Gemma said.

"Yeah, he's pretty amazing," Patrick agreed and chuckled. "I feel really blessed to be his dad."

"What was his mother like?" Gemma asked, softly.

Patrick could feel the same defensiveness he'd felt at the diner begin to rear up inside him, but he forced it back down. Guess he'd have to get used to answering questions about Lucy now.

"I don't know how to answer that," he said, honestly. "Because I don't know if my memories of her are colored by who I hoped she could be, instead of who she actually was. She was like…" His voice trailed off for a moment as he searched his mind for a metaphor. Gemma waited for him to find his words. "She was like a butterfly—pretty and constantly in motion, flitting from one person to another."

"And when she settled on you, it made you feel special?" Gemma asked, softly. "Even if it was only for a moment?"

"Yeah," Patrick admitted. Huh, he'd never really thought of it like that. "I bought my first house when I was nineteen. It was a total rundown shack and needed a lot of work. Basically, got it for nothing. We started dating, and the next thing I knew, she was living with me on and off. I must've proposed to her a hundred times. I wanted to marry her, and I even bought her a diamond ring. I wanted to do things right, especially after Tristan was born."

He'd grown up believing that he could fix anything, and that if he just tried a little harder he could make things work.

"She never wanted to be a wife or a mother," he went on. "I hoped that she'd change after Tristan was born. But she kept drifting away. She'd leave me for days and weeks at a time, going off with various people she'd meet at the bar. When I asked her where she was going, she'd just yell at me and tell me she didn't love me. Last thing she told me was that she and her friend Missy were going to meet up with Missy's boyfriend and go to a big Christmas party."

"Was Missy short for anything?" Gemma asked.

Like maybe Marissa?

He shook his head. "Not that I know of."

"Did this boyfriend have a name?"

"They called him Angel, but I think that was a nickname."

"Where was this party?"

"I don't know," Patrick said, "but near North Bay, which is pretty close to Noëlville. She said something about making easy money. But I never got details. I begged her to stay and be there for Tristan's first Christmas. She told me she was never coming back. But she said that a lot and I didn't believe her."

"And then she never returned," Gemma said. "Did you call the police and report her missing?"

He blew out a harsh breath.

"In a town like Juniper Cove, everyone knows everybody's else's business," he said. "It was no secret that she cheated on me and the whole island knew she'd finally up and left."

At least that was what he'd told himself at the time. But maybe his pride had been hurting so badly he hadn't even considered she could be in trouble. "Now I'm wishing I had tried to find her," he admitted.

"Did Lucy work?" Gemma asked.

"Some waitressing. All cash under the table."

"Any criminal history?"

"Theft," Patrick admitted. "Small stuff."

Gemma had told him back at the diner that sometimes people who had information on cold cases had reasons not to want to talk to police. Missy and her boyfriend might fall into that camp.

"So, it's possible she and Missy have something to do with the stash the men in hats are looking for," Gemma said. "Although if so, it would've been stolen a long time ago, and we're probably looking for a more recent theft. I'm also wondering if Missy is the Marissa whose wallet was found on Lucy's body."

"It's possible," Patrick conceded.

"The weirdest thing to me about this whole situation," Gemma went on, "is the bell tattoo. All of the Noëlville victims had a bell tattoo, and now you're saying that Lucy got that tattoo months before she disappeared in order to commemorate Tristan's birth. Which throws our entire hypothesis about it being the killer's trademark out of the window. The only possible explanation I can think of is that our killer or killers noticed Lucy's tattoo then and decided to mark all of their victims with it. But why? The whole thing is fishy."

Gemma took a long sip of her apple cider, and Patrick realized he hadn't touched his. He reached down, broke one of the cookies in half and popped it in his mouth. He chased it down with a sip of cider, which singed his tongue. And while his brain told him that the cookie was chewy and the cider smelled like cinnamon, they both tasted like ash in his mouth.

"It's important to me that you and I are on the same page before my team arrives in the morning," Gemma said. "Or at least that you know where I'm coming from. So far, my working theory is that Missy is Marissa Kerry. It shouldn't take my team too long to prove it, one way or another. I'm guessing Lucy and Missy ran into some kind of trouble—maybe due to whatever they were doing at this party. Then Lucy was killed. But because she had Marissa's driver's license on her, her body was misidentified until now."

She set her cup down and turned to him. Her blue eyes locked on his face—she was so incredibly attractive and intelligent, yet kind too—and it was like something in the depths of her gaze tugged at his heart. No, he couldn't let himself be drawn to Gemma this way.

Not because there was anything wrong with her, at least as far as he could tell. But because clearly something about his own heart was fundamentally broken. First, he'd had a child with a woman who'd treated both him and his son like garbage. Then Gemma's own task force had discovered Patrick's best friend was a killer. How could he have read them so wrong?

Seemed that some people just weren't good judges of character. What if he committed to someone only to find out he was wrong and get his heart broken again. Only this time, Tristan could get hurt too.

He broke her gaze, looked down and realized that their knees were barely inches away from each other.

"I have absolutely no clue how the Noëlville Serial Killer fits into any of this," Gemma said, "or Rust, Bone and Umber."

Something she'd said in the diner flickered across his mind.

With a serial killer like that, it's all about creating fear...

A loud bang shook the air as the power went out, plunging them into near darkness. Gemma leaped to her feet, so did he, and suddenly he found himself reaching for her. His hands brushed her arms. Her fingers clutched the sleeves of his shirt. Then his eyes adjusted to the low light from the fire behind him.

"Sounded like a tree came down and took out the power lines!" Gemma let go and stepped back. He did too. "I've got a generator in the garage. I'll go get it started."

"I need to go check on Tristan." Patrick's heart was pounding so hard in his chest he struggled to breathe.

Why had he reached for Gemma like that? Why had she reached for him?

She walked to the back door and slid on her boots and jacket.

"Don't go outside alone," he added.

"I don't have to," she said. "There's an internal door to the garage. I'll be back in a moment."

"Okay." He turned and started up the spiral staircase to the second floor, using the flashlight on his phone.

He heard the door open and close as Gemma slipped through into the garage.

"Hey, buddy?" he called as he jogged down the landing. "You okay?"

No answer. Patrick opened the bedroom door to feel a cold wind rush up to meet him. He scanned the space. The room was empty. But the wardrobe was open and had been rummaged through. The window looked out onto a slanted roof that covered the length of the back porch. Fresh sneaker footprints tracked across it all the way to the edge and then reappeared down on the snowy driveway below.

The air froze in his chest.

"Tristan?" Patrick leaned out the window and shouted into the storm. "Tristan, where are you?"

A single trail of footprints led away from the cottage. An engine revved, a light flickered through the gloom, and he saw the car. For a fleeting moment, he could see his son sitting in the front seat, in the faint glow of the car's interior light. It looked like his son was arguing with a hooded figure behind the wheel.

"Tristan!" Patrick shouted his son's name into the storm. "Get out of there!"

But it was too late. A gun appeared in the driver's hand aimed at his preteen son. The car shot forward into the night.

Tristan had been taken.

FIVE

"No!" The single panicked word exploded through Patrick's core. "Tristan!"

Instinctively, he threw his body through the open window, landing with his bare hands and stockinged feet on the slanted overhang. He scrambled down the tiles, ignoring the biting cold cutting into his body. The car was disappearing through the trees with Tristan inside. But he wasn't about to let them take his child. Not without a fight.

He hit the ground and tumbled into a mixture of slush and snow. Judging by the footprints on the ground, it looked like his son had grabbed sneakers from the bedroom cupboard. Hopefully he'd grabbed a coat too.

And here Patrick was only in his shirtsleeves and socks.

Judging by the single line of footprints it looked like Tristan had been alone when he'd left the cottage, and somebody had snatched him from the driveway. But why had his son snuck out? What had he been doing? What had he been thinking? A barrage of questions pounded through his brain, but he didn't have time to stop and think. Let alone go back for his coat, boots and Gemma's help. He could only run after the departing car. Hoping against all fleeting glimpses of hope that somehow he'd be able to stop it, pull Tristan out, rescue him and bring him to safety. He glanced at his phone, and it still didn't have a signal.

"Gemma!" he shouted, not knowing if there was any way she could even hear him. "I need your car!"

But any hope of chasing after Tristan's abductor was immediately dashed when he reached her car and saw that someone had slashed all four tires.

Whoever had taken his son wanted to make sure of a clean getaway and that they wouldn't be able to chase after him. And now, they were stranded.

He ran forward, pushing his body down the snow-covered road and through the trees, ignoring the piercing pain that filled his chest and spread through his limbs, until they were numb.

But the taillights got smaller and smaller as they disappeared into the distance. Until finally, they were gone entirely. Even then he kept running in vain, hoping that if he just kept pushing himself hard enough he'd catch a glimpse of the car again and be able to save his son. But the darkness surrounding him was so deep he could barely see his hand in front of his face. It swallowed him.

That's when the fear and sorrow hit him full force, crashing over his body like a wave and buckling his legs beneath him. He sunk to his knees in the snow.

Lord, I have no choice but to place my son into Your loving hands and trust in You to keep him safe. Please protect him from all enemies that would hurt him. Please surround him with Your shield of defense. Please speak to his heart and give him Your wisdom. Please help me find him and bring him home safely.

For a long moment, he knelt there, feeling the snow beat against his neck and the wind lash his body. Then he stood, turned and started walking back the way he'd come, trying to retrace his steps the best he could, in the direction he hoped would lead him to Gemma's cottage.

He was the only parent Tristan had ever known. The one and only person in this world his son had been able to count on. Now his son had been snatched right out from under his nose—what was more, it seemed Tristan had walked right into danger without his own father having any clue.

Patrick hadn't seen what he'd needed to about what his own son had been going through. He'd let Tristan down. All he could do was hold on to the belief that one day he'd see his son again.

And that he wouldn't just vanish like his mother once had.

No, no, he wouldn't let himself fear the worst.

He'd find Gemma and tell her everything that happened. She'd help him get his head on straight and focus on every salient fact he needed to remember in order to find his son. Once the phone lines came back, the province would put out an Amber Alert. Then, in a few hours, the sun would rise, the roads would clear, her team would arrive and together they'd strategize a plan to rescue and locate the boy.

He wasn't alone. There were people who'd help him find his son.

And for now, he'd cling to that glimmer of hope with all the strength that he had.

He stuck to the road, trusting that to keep him from getting lost. At least five inches of snow had fallen since the storm had hit. For a long moment, nothing but pitch black swarmed him, as the blizzard roiled under a cloud-filled sky. Then finally, a tiny yellow speck glowed in the distance. He'd found the cottage, and it looked like Gemma had succeeded in starting the generator and getting the lights back on. He jogged toward it, his body longing for the warmth and shelter that lay just beyond the door.

But it was still just a glimmer in the trees, as the sound of Simcoe barking furiously filled the air. Then came another sound that sent a fresh chill through his veins—Gemma was screaming for help.

"Gemma!"

He abandoned the road and ran straight through the trees, keeping his eyes locked at the yellow beacon of light leading him back to her. For a long moment her screams filled the air. They were angry, defiant and terrified. Then two pops rang out in the darkness—gunshots—and then just as suddenly her voice stopped. That scared him even more than her cries.

"Gemma!" he shouted. "Are you alright? I'm coming! Hang on!"

Lord, please may she be alright. Help me reach her in time.

Had there been a secondary attack on Gemma, while he'd been chasing after Tristan's kidnappers? Had it been coordinated? If so, he'd fallen straight into their trap. Why hadn't he at least tried to shout to her to let her know what was going on before chasing after Tristan's kidnappers? He'd been too focused on getting to his son to consider she might be in danger too.

Gemma's voice had vanished completely, but Simcoe's barking still rose—loud, furious and like a battle cry directing Patrick back. Finally, the cottage came into view fully.

He scanned the area and didn't see Gemma anywhere. Then he ran for the door—it was locked. For a moment, he banged his fists on the door, rattled the doorknob and yelled for Gemma. But there was no answer. He gave up and ran around the side of the building looking for another way in. The garage door was ajar. That's where Gemma had gone to start the generator. He ducked inside and immediately saw signs of a struggle. Crates and boxes of sports gear and hardware supplies had been tipped over. Oars and life jackets had been yanked from shelves. A hamper of laundry had toppled over beside the washing machine, and a ski rack hung sideways, having been half torn from the wall.

Whatever had happened to Gemma, she'd fought for her life and hadn't given up without a struggle. Patrick could hear Simcoe throwing herself against the interior door that led to the cottage. Thankfully, Gemma had left it unlocked, although she'd left Simcoe inside. He yanked it open, and Simcoe barreled into him, nearly knocking him over. The kelpie leaped up on her hind legs, pressing her front paw against Patrick's chest and howling at him urgently.

"I got it," he said. "Gemma's in trouble, she's gone and we need to help her."

There were no new tire tracks in the driveway and he'd have noticed a departing car. So, somebody had dragged her off on foot. Not that he could make out much in the way of a distinct footprint trail thanks to the mess of freshly fallen snow.

His heart was still bursting to find his son. But the evidence and his experience also told him he was far more likely to be successful in rescuing Gemma right now. Plus, something in his gut told him that he'd then have a much better chance of finding and rescuing Tristan if he had Gemma by his side.

His phone still didn't have a signal, and for now he was in no state to launch a successful rescue mission. Patrick went inside and yanked off his soaking wet socks. His skin was bright red and felt like it was on fire from the sudden shift of temperature. He found a pair of thick men's wool socks in the dryer, put them on and sprinted for her front door, with Simcoe tight at his heels. Within seconds, he'd shoved on his jacket, boots and gloves as well. Then he turned to the K-9. The kelpie was hovering beside him and yipping anxiously, as if reminding him to go faster.

"Okay," Patrick said. "Where is she? Take me to Gemma."

Simcoe's head tilted to the side as if trying to figure out what he was asking of her.

"I'm sorry, I don't speak K-9." Patrick bent down until he and Simcoe were eye level. "But it's an emergency and I need to find Gemma."

The dog sat and whimpered slightly. She didn't understand.

Help me, Lord. I can't find Gemma on my own. Simcoe is my only hope. Please help me get through to her.

A splash of blue to his left drew his eye. It was Gemma's scarf. He pulled it off the peg where she'd left it and held it in front of Simcoe's nose.

"You know Gemma? This belongs to Gemma."

For a moment the dog looked at it quizzically. Patrick prayed that somehow—despite the fact Simcoe had never been taught to follow his commands and he'd never been trained how to give them—the dog would realize what Patrick was asking him to do. He picked up Simcoe's K-9 vest, helped the dog step into it and clipped it on. Then he held the scarf under Simcoe's nose again.

"You're back on duty," Patrick said. "We're in this together. You and me. Gemma's in trouble, and we're all she's got. Please, go find Gemma. Show me where Gemma is."

Simcoe sniffed the scarf. Then her ears perked and she gave a sharp and triumphant bark. Simcoe turned, then ran across the living room and through the door into the garage. There the dog paused and sniffed again. Hope leaped in Patrick's chest, and he glanced around for a makeshift weapon.

Then the dog dashed out the door and into the snow.

Gemma's kidnapper was carrying her over his shoulder like a sack of potatoes. Umber and Bone had pulled a burlap bag over her head and tied her hands together at the wrists as well. Considering the fight she'd put up against the two of them when they'd rushed her in the garage, she guessed she should be thankful they hadn't tied her feet as well, considering they didn't seem willing to let her walk. If they were carrying her because they assumed she'd run away if she was on her feet—they'd be right.

She went limp to preserve her strength and listened to the sounds of footsteps crunching in the snow and the wind shaking the trees. She was completely blinded by the bag and knew that the only thing keeping her from feeling the full impact of the fear now coursing through her veins was her own stubborn determination to keep fighting for her life just as soon as somebody gave her the opportunity.

But even as she prayed that God would save her life, send someone to find her and show her when to act, she could feel an even deeper worry about Patrick and Tristan creeping at the edges of her mind.

Where were they? Had something happened to them? They hadn't come when they'd heard her screaming for help. Had the kidnappers gotten to them first?

She thought she'd heard some kind of muffled shout coming from outside when she'd been fighting with the generator and trying to get it going. But it had been almost impossible to hear much over the whiz of the chain pull and rumble of the motor, as it tried to catch before spluttering out again. Then the generator had roared to life, the lights had come on, the power had been back—and then two men had struck her before she'd even had the opportunity to run.

And now, here she was, being carried through the woods to who-knew-where, by the man she guessed was Umber while presumably Bone walked beside them, keeping a gun trained on her in case she tried anything funny. She had no idea where Rust was.

She willed her brain to think, to keep her emotions at bay so they couldn't overwhelm. This was a puzzle—a deadly and urgent one—but that didn't mean she couldn't crack it.

Why were they on foot right now? Where was the men's car? Presumably they'd parked a ways away from the cottage in order to sneak up on her. But why? And where were they taking her? Why wasn't she down on her knees in the snow right now, like Patrick had been, with a gun pressed against her head while they demanded to know where the so-called stash was? Did they think she didn't know? Or was the opposite true and they were thinking she'd take them to it?

The footsteps stopped, and she could hear Umber and Bone arguing. Bone was telling Umber to stay there with her while he went to talk to someone and get the car. That must mean they weren't far from the road. She couldn't make out everything they were saying, but it sounded like Umber wasn't too thrilled at being left alone in the woods on babysitting duty. Did Umber have a gun too? She assumed so but hadn't seen it, and for now his hands were too busy lugging her around to pull it.

She heard Bone walk off through the woods. His footsteps grew quieter until they faded completely. She wondered if Umber was going to put her down, but instead he shifted her position over her shoulder, until she felt what seemed to be his shoulder press against her ear. Okay, that would work too.

Lord, save me now...

She turned her head toward what she assumed to be his neck and bit down as hard as she could through the burlap sack, not even sure if he'd feel it between the cloth and the collar of his overcoat. Immediately, she realized she'd needn't have worried. Umber bellowed and hurled her away from him. For a terrifying second she flew backward through the air. Then her body smacked hard against the ground. She struggled to get up to her feet, as her boots slid on the slippery ground and her hands were still tied behind her back.

For a fleeting moment she actually thought she'd manage to stand, but she lost her footing and fell back to the ground again. A sharp and piercing pain shot through her arm as she felt Umber step down hard on her shoulder, pushing her down into the ground, and she suspected it was only the snow that kept it from breaking. She yelped in pain.

"Let me be clear!" Umber shouted. "The only reason you're still alive, Missy, is because we need that stash. But we will do anything it takes to get it, even if it means tearing you limb from limb!"

Help...me... Lord...

A burst of furious barking filled the air. Footsteps pelted toward them through the snow. Simcoe? Then a strong and unmistakable voice reached her ears through the haze of darkness and pain.

"Leave her alone!"

Patrick!

He was there. He was coming for her, and he wasn't going to let them take her.

Gemma still couldn't see anything in the pitch-black darkness that surrounded her. But she knew that Patrick and Simcoe were running through the woods. They were coming to rescue her. The sound of barking turned into a furious snarl. Umber swore loudly in pain. The pressure suddenly left her arm. Violent, angry threats bombarded her ears as Umber shouted in terrible detail just how badly he was about to hurt her and Patrick. Then a crack split the air and Umber's yelling stopped.

An indistinct cacophony of sounds filled her ears, leaving her to only guess what was happening now. Simcoe growled. Branches broke. Footsteps now ran away from her through the woods. Simcoe's growling faded and the K-9's comforting warmth pressed up against her body, letting Gemma know she wasn't completely alone. A distant engine roared.

Then the very faint sound of Patrick shouting rose on the wind.

"Where... Is... My... Son?"

A painful shiver ran through Gemma's body that pierced even deeper than the cold around her.

Had she heard that right? Had something happened to Tristan?

Moments later, she heard footsteps approaching again.

"It's okay, Gemma," Patrick called. His voice was equal parts reassuring, concerned and urgent. "I'm here. You're safe now. But we've got to run."

She felt as Patrick knelt down beside her. His fingers brushed her injured shoulder. Then gently, he pulled the hood from her head and then brushed a gloved hand along the side of her cheek. She looked up. His face hovered over hers. "Are you okay? Can you stand?"

"Yeah," she said. "I think so."

He reached one arm around her back, supporting her in a half hug as he freed her wrists. She looked around. They appeared to be alone. She couldn't see Tristan either.

"Where's Tristan?" she asked. "Is he okay?"

Patrick didn't answer right away, and she had the worrying suspicion that she'd been right in what she'd heard, and now Patrick was stalling. He slid one hand under her elbow, placed the other on the small of her back and helped her up to her feet.

"We'll talk once we're safe."

They started walking quickly, side by side, through the snow back to the cottage.

In her line of work, Gemma knew more than a little about

what it was like when a person went into a fight or flight mode. It was a survival technique All thoughts, feelings, emotional reactions and even physical sensations got put on hold, except for the one basic and urgent desire to get somewhere safe and fast. And something in the way Patrick's intense gaze cut straight ahead through the dark forest, made her fear that was happening to him now.

The memory of his desperate shout cut through her mind. *Where is my son?*

"Patrick, what happened?"

"Simcoe bit Umber's leg," Patrick said. His hand brushed her back again, steering her toward the faint glimmer of the cottage lights. "Then I smacked him right in the face with a canoe paddle."

Gemma opened her mouth, but no words came out.

"That man will be fine," he went on, "He ran, I saw headlights through the trees, then I heard him hop into a car and I lost him. I figure that means we've got a very small head start before they catch up with us again. Not much, but better than nothing." His footstep quickened and so did hers. "How many men did you see?"

"Two," she said. "Bone and Umber jumped me in the garage. Bone did say something about getting a car, so there might just be the two of them. I didn't see Rust." She glanced back over her shoulder. It didn't seem like they were being followed on foot and considering how the cottage road curved, she and Patrick would barely make it back to the cottage before the men in the car did. "He called me Missy and asked me where the stash was. Maybe he thinks I'm Lucy's friend and that's who robbed them... What happened to you and Tristan?"

"We're going to need a plan," Patrick said ignoring her

question, "and unfortunately they've flattened the tires on your car, so—"

"Patrick." She cut him off. "Where is Tristan?" When he didn't answer immediately she reached out and grabbed his arm. Yes, the fact her car had been sabotaged mattered—everything mattered—but not as much as knowing why Patrick wasn't answering her question about his son. "Tell me what's going on. Is he okay?"

Patrick didn't meet her eyes. "Tristan was kidnapped."

It was just a three-word answer, and yet pain swelled in his voice until it broke.

She stopped suddenly. Her hand tightened on his arm. "What do you mean, he's been kidnapped?" She turned back toward the way they'd come. "We have to go help him."

Patrick stopped too, his whole body turned to her, and although his face was shrouded in snow and darkness, there was no mistaking the desperate emotion filling his voice.

"We can't," he said, "Not until we figure out where he is. Whoever kidnapped him took him by car—maybe a few minutes before you were attacked by Bone and Umber. Maybe Rust took him. I don't know. I didn't see. I chased after the car on foot until I lost sight of it. Right now, there's nothing we can do but get ourselves to safety and marshal help." He took her hand and clutched it tightly in his. "I've got to get you to safety before it's too late."

Patrick's fingers looped through hers and squeezed. She squeezed him back, and then they kept running, side by side, through the trees. As they neared the cottage, they slowed to catch their breath, and he told her the rest of the story. About finding Tristan's room empty and his son's tracks to the woods, the hooded person in the car. But his story came out in jumbled bits of information between deep breaths, like a jigsaw puzzle she had to put together in her own mind with many of the pieces still missing. Had Tristan been kidnapped by Rust or someone else? Why had Tristan snuck out the window to meet someone? Did that mean he knew them? Or thought he did?

Together, Gemma, Patrick and Simcoe hurried through the garage and into the cottage, locking the doors behind them. And only then did Gemma let go of Patrick's hand. Almost immediately she missed the strength and warmth that had seemed to emanate from his grasp.

"Okay, so what do we do?" Patrick glanced around the living room, taking in the space before his eyes then fixed on her face. "Your car isn't going to get us very far with four flat tires in a snowstorm, but I'm willing to try it if that's all that separates us from three angry men with weapons intent on taking us out."

"And apparently they have a car," Gemma added, "maybe two, which means they'll be able to outrun us pretty easily."

"Do we have access to another vehicle?" Patrick said. "A snowmobile? A neighbor's vehicle? Anything? Or do we just try to hunker down in here, fortify the best we can and wait for rescue?"

She looked around the cottage as if seeing it for the first time with new eyes.

The open-concept main room with floor-to-ceiling windows had always flooded the room with sunlight and given her a dazzling view of the lake. But it also made them achingly vulnerable to attacks.

"The windows are reinforced glass," she said, "which is great for storms but not exactly the same as bulletproof."

"Is there somewhere we fortify ourselves inside?" he asked.

"The only main floor room that doesn't have a direct exit to the outside is my niece Skye's nursery."

Was it her imagination or was there the faint sound of a motor outside the cottage now? Immediately, she switched off the lights and stepped close enough to the window that she could look out. At first, there was nothing but darkness and silence. Then, flashlights flickered in the trees.

She turned back to Patrick and felt the color drain from her face. "They're here."

Help us, Lord, what do we do?

They needed a good option, but all she could feel were lousy possibilities cascading through her mind. They could run through the forest to the neighbors' empty cottage in the hopes of finding a vehicle. They could try to escape on foot through the trees. They could hide and wait for rescue. But the men in fedoras had the advantage, and every option ran the risk of getting caught before they got far. Or worse, being killed.

There has to be another way. Lord, what am I not seeing? What possible advantage do we have?

Then it hit her.

"We have a boat and they don't!" she exclaimed and turned to Patrick. "They can follow us on foot or on the road, but they can't follow us across the lake."

"The lake is frozen!" Patrick said.

"But the boathouse is heated." Gemma was already grabbing a strong rucksack and tossing in enough basic supplies to get them through a few hours—an emergency camping kit, blankets, flares, matches and water. Then she added the gingerbread cookies and Tristan's things. "It's only frozen around the shore and the islands. We'll have to be really careful because there are a lot of hidden rocks. But if we can break through the ice, we can take the boat across the lake and they won't be able to follow us."

From there, they could find a place to hide out, maybe even

call for help and report Tristan's abduction if they could get closer to town. Maybe someone in the town of Cedar Lake had access to a four-wheel truck. Either way, they couldn't stay here. She'd lived on her own off the grid for almost two weeks in the past when on the run from a killer who'd wanted her dead. They could survive the night.

"What do you need?" Patrick's voice came from somewhere behind her.

"Anything you want to add to my rucksack and something to break the ice with."

"Like these?"

She turned back. He was holding a fire poker in one hand and an axe in the other. Both were wrapped in gold and green ribbon and had been sitting in a bronze bucket beside the fire.

"Those should do it." A determined smile crossed her lips. "Now it's just a matter of getting to the boat."

Seconds later, they'd finished loading her rucksack and bundling up to go out in the cold. Then came the tricky part—getting to the boat without being spotted. The last thing she wanted was to get into a fight for her life on the way to her boat. Thankfully, it seemed the men in fedoras were still biding their time outside the cottage instead of launching an attack or breaking their way in. Carefully, she crept around the cottage from window to window, staying low and following the glow of their flashlights and snippets of conversation as they moved around the building. Silently Patrick followed. Finally, she stopped and peered out the back door window and watched as the men stopped outside the same garage door where they'd initially broken in to kidnap her.

"What are they doing?" Patrick asked.

He was at her shoulder and Simcoe was pressed up against her leg.

"I don't know," she whispered. "Maybe they figured that's

the easiest way in and don't realize the reinforced inner door will stop them from getting any further."

"Or maybe they're waiting for instructions from someone?" Patrick suggested.

She turned toward him, her shoulder brushed his, and something tightened in her chest when she realized they'd been standing so close. There was something protective in his stance. Almost like he was instinctively sheltering her from the enemy even before they struck.

"I think we should make a run for it," she said, "and hope they don't realize we're gone until it's too late."

He nodded. "Sounds good."

Patrick slung the rucksack over both shoulders and fastened it across his chest. She took the fire poker from his hands and signaled Simcoe to stay by her side, then together they moved to the sliding glass door that overlooked the lake. Carefully, she pressed her palm against the glass and slid it open. It squeaked softly. Cold air and heavy flakes whipped at her face. She held her breath and looked out over the long stretch of ground that led from the front porch to the lake. Shadowy trees framed them on both sides. She couldn't even see the boathouse in the darkness.

There were no men in fedoras or flashlights in sight, but she knew they couldn't be far. She took a deep breath and let it out slowly.

"Help us, Lord," she whispered.

"Amen," Patrick said. His hand brushed her shoulder, and the simple gesture seemed to fill her with strength. Then he said, "Okay, let's go."

Silently, Gemma, Patrick and Simcoe slipped out through the open glass door and into the night. She slid the door behind them, wincing at the beeping sound the buttons made as she locked the door and armed the security system. Then together they ran down the porch steps, over to the tree line and down toward the water, moving single file with Gemma taking the lead, Simcoe in the middle and Patrick following behind. And of all the thousands of times she'd run down from the cottage to the lake, it had never felt this long. Let alone dangerous.

They reached the boathouse, she unlocked the door, and they ran inside and closed the door behind them. The faint sound of water lapping filled her ears. Patrick shone his flashlight over the family motorboat, then yanked the winter cover off while she lowered the boat down the ramp into the water and then slowly opened the garage-style door that led out into the lake. Patrick slid the beam of his flashlight through the open door and out onto the ice that lay before them.

It was at least two inches thick and stretched out a good fifteen feet before giving way to open waters. More thick rings of ice surrounded the dozens of tiny islands that dotted Cedar Lake. Patrick tossed the rucksack in the motorboat, heaved the axe over his shoulder, walked over to the open door and swung down hard into the ice. A loud crack split the air as a patch of ice shattered under the impact.

"How loud is the motor?" Patrick asked.

"Pretty quiet while it's idling," Gemma said. "But when I throw the throttle it's a roar."

And they wanted to stay as quiet as they could for as long as possible to keep the men from noticing their escape.

"Alright, you get in," Patrick said. "Start the motor. I'll keep chipping away from here until you can maneuver it out. Unfortunately, breaking the ice is going to be a lot louder than I hoped."

"How are you being so calm right now?" she asked.

His jaw set. "Panicking never helped anyone."

True. Silently, she thanked God that a Jack of All Rescue Trades was the man by her side. She climbed in and signaled to Simcoe, who leaped over the edge of the boat and in beside her. Then she leaned over the left side of the boat and thwacked away at the ice in front of her with the poker. It chipped slowly and took far more effort than she'd have hoped. But finally, when there was no more ice within her reach, she started the engine.

It coughed and spluttered, releasing a thin whisp of smoke into the dark and freezing air, before it died again.

Patrick leaped in. "Everything okay?"

"It's too cold to start," she said. "The engine needs a second to warm up."

She grabbed an oar, reached overboard and pushed the boat out of the boathouse. They inched forward. The metal bow screeched as it rubbed against the ice. She stood at the wheel and used the oar to push them out into the water. Patrick climbed onto the bow and crouched down, balancing himself precariously on the balls of his feet while he continued to swing the axe down, to break a path free in front of them. Slowly, they crept out of the boathouse and into the lake beyond, until they'd lost even the modest shelter of the boathouse walls.

She tried the engine again. This time it caught with a sudden jolt. Ice splintered and the boat lurched forward into open water. Patrick lost his footing and grabbed ahold of the boat's windscreen to keep from falling.

Angry voices rose on the wind. She looked back over her shoulder. Three men were running through the snow toward them, their silhouettes illuminated by the flashlights in their hands.

"Be careful," Gemma shouted, "and get in!"

Patrick scrambled into the back of the motorboat. She yanked back on the throttle and the engine roared. The boat began to pick up speed as it shot across the water to the darkened shore on the other side. She risked one more glance back in the direction of the cottage and wondered if this was the last time she'd ever see it again. She turned back to the lake.

During the summer, there were buoys and markers to direct her safely across the lake. Now cold and darkness had turned it into an obstacle course of hidden dangers. Icy rocks and islands seemed to loom out of the darkness with perilous jagged edges. Spinning slabs of ice seemed to almost lunge across the water at them. Then came the sound of gunshots, as the men fired their weapons at the departing boat. She heard the clang of a bullet ricocheting off the side of the boat, then the splashes of bullets hitting the water.

Suddenly, her hands froze on the wheel as terrifying memories swept through her mind, of being run off the road by a killer firing his gun at her, of crashing off the bridge into the water and thinking she was going to drown.

"Watch out!" Patrick said.

Then she felt the boat smash hard against something she couldn't see. A rock? A large chunk of ice? The boat spun sideways. She'd lost control of the wheel, and Patrick reached past her to grab it. She stumbled back.

"Sit down!" Patrick called.

But it was too late. The boat jolted hard again. For a moment, she could feel it rocking wildly beneath her feet. Then she pitched over the side, her head smacked against the gunwale, and her body hit the water. The cold hit her with a sudden shock and she sunk into the icy depths below.

SIX

The blow from the frigid water overwhelmed her, paralyzing her and filling her veins with a cold so intense it seemed to burn her from the inside like fire. Her body dropped fast, sinking like a stone, weighed down by her heavy winter gear and boots. Darkness filled her eyes and surrounded her on all sides. Her lungs screamed for air. She thrashed wildly, trying to regain control of her limbs, unable for a moment to even figure out which direction to swim to even reach the surface.

Save me, Lord!

Then she saw a beam of light dancing above her and to her right. Her heart leaped. Patrick was searching for her.

She swam toward the light, pulling her body through the water with every ounce of strength she had.

Her hands broke through the surface, then her fingers smashed hard against what felt like a thin but solid concrete slab. She was trapped beneath one of the large slabs of ice! Desperately she treaded water and pushed up hard against it with both hands, gasping for shallow breaths in the narrow sliver of air that appeared whenever she managed to lift it. It was light enough to lift, but solid too, without any cracks or holes to break her way through. Urgently, she pushed again but couldn't find the edge or any way out.

Her limbs grew weak. She wasn't going to make it.

The flashlight beam danced across the ice above her, filling her eyes with shimmering golden light. A shadow moved on the surface, and she looked up to see Patrick's silhouette, standing on the boat above her.

"Hang on!" he shouted, but his voice was muffled, like it was coming from a very long way away. "I'm coming!"

For a split second, the shape of Patrick seemed to grow larger, looming tall above her. The fire poker rose high before plunging down near her. A resounding crack filled the air, the ice shattered and the water churned suddenly as Patrick plunged through the frozen water beside her. She gasped a deep breath as the ice disappeared above her, she was pulled from the water and fresh air filled her lungs again. Then she felt Patrick tug her into his chest and hold her to him, and she realized he'd had the wherewithal to put on a life jacket.

"It's okay." His breath was ragged in her ear. His hands wrapped around her waist. "I've got you."

"Thank you." She tried to reach up and slide her arms around his neck, but her fingers were so cold that all she could do was curl them around the straps on the front of his life jacket.

Thick snow blew against her face. The world had fallen silent now except for the wind whistling past them and the water lapping against unseen rocks. Inky black air surrounded them on all sides, as if they were floating in a void.

"Where's the boat?" Her teeth were chattering so hard she could barely get the words out.

"It can't be far." Patrick was looking around. "The moment you went overboard, I yanked the emergency stop cord, cut the engine and dropped anchor."

He eased his one hand away from her, and she realized he'd managed to tuck his flashlight in a loop of his life jacket before grabbing her. He'd done the same with her fire poker.

That must be weighting him down. He held the flashlight up and flicked the switch. The light spluttered yellow for a moment and died.

She clung tighter to Patrick. Her fingers felt so stiff she could barely bend them. "Where's Simcoe?"

"In the boat." Now Patrick's teeth were chattering too. "She tried to jump in after you, but I hauled her back and told her to stay."

"Simcoe..." She tried to yell, but her voice barely rose above a weak mewl. "Speak..."

"Simcoe!" Patrick shouted, and his voice strained as he forced it through his frosty breath. Then he struck two fingers in his mouth and whistled. The high-pitched noise seemed to crack the night air.

A sharp, urgent and enthusiastic barking sounded back in response.

Gemma breathed a sigh of relief. Slowly and painfully, she and Patrick swam toward Simcoe as the dog called to them. Then she could see the silhouette of the boat in the darkness. Patrick reached for it with the end of the fire poker and pulled it to them. Then Patrick guided her hands to the ladder he'd left suspended over the side. She could barely climb. Her hands felt too weak to hold the ropes. The rungs slipped under her feet. Patrick helped her over the edge, and she tumbled onto the boat floor. It was only then that she saw Patrick had kicked off his boots before coming for her and must've swum in his bare feet. A weak smile crossed her lips. He wasn't half-bad in a crisis. It was a nice quality.

But now that she was out of the water, somehow the cold cut even deeper than before, and her whole body shook. The boat rocked as the blizzard whipped faster. Patrick pulled a blanket from the rucksack and draped it over her.

"Just hold on, okay?" Concern filled his voice as he

crouched down in front of her. Simcoe nestled beside her, and Gemma couldn't tell if Patrick had signaled her to or if the dog was acting on instinct.

"I'm going to get us to shore and find somewhere warm," Patrick went on. "We're not going to last much longer out here, especially if the storm gets worse. I'm just a little turned around right now and can't tell where we are, and which direction is which. Any suggestions?"

She glanced over the gunwale but saw nothing but darkness and snow in all directions. She was lost, in the lake where she'd swum thousands of times, and now she could feel a heavy, cold sleepiness like she'd never felt before sweeping over her body. Her eyes closed. Simcoe snuggled closer. The boat rocked beneath her. A spray of water washed over the side.

She opened her eyes again, to see that Patrick had put his shoes and socks back on and was now rowing through the water with an oar, to avoid running into anything else, and navigating carefully around obstacles she couldn't see. Did that mean they were close to shore? And had she actually answered Patrick's question? Or shaken her head? She didn't actually know. It felt like every time her eyes closed they stayed shut for longer and longer, and the drowsiness was growing heavier.

The boat jolted and then shuttered to a stop. Her eyes opened again, and now she could see the outline of trees.

"Where are we?" she asked.

"I don't know." Patrick crouched down in front of her again. "But there's some kind of building over there, and anything is better than being out on the lake in this storm. Can you walk?"

She nodded and tried to tell him that she thought so, but the words failed to make it past her frozen lips, and when he slid his arm under her shoulders to help her to her feet, she felt her legs buckle weakly beneath her.

"I'll take that as a no." There was a positivity and warmth in Patrick's voice. No doubt his way of trying to reassure her that everything was going to be okay. Maybe reassure them both. He kept on talking to her as he swept her up into her arms and held her so snuggly against him that she could feel his heartbeat through their coats. He told her over and over again that she was fine, she was going to be okay, and that she needed to stay awake and would be warm again soon. She clung to his voice like an anchor, pulling her back to consciousness every time she felt her mind drifting away.

Gemma was vaguely aware of him leaping out of the boat onto rocks with her in his arms, steadying himself and calling to Simcoe. Then Patrick was trudging up a slope, with the sound of snow crunching under his feet and Simcoe running beside him. His movements were slow, he kept readjusting his arms, and she suspected he was carrying the rucksack, probably with the poker and axe both attached to it. A few more uneven steps, and suddenly they were out of the storm and she could hear his footsteps creaking on what sounded like well-worn wooden floorboards. He shifted the weight of her in his arms, then rusty hinges squeaked and the whistle of the wind changed as it moved through the cracks of whatever door they'd come through.

"Now, I'm just going to set you down while I make you a fire so we can warm up, okay?" Patrick said, and although his upbeat tone didn't falter, she could hear the deep and unmistakable sound of worry moving through his voice.

She wanted to open her eyes, to respond to him and to tell him that she was fine. But it was like her brain had floated away from her body, leaving it behind. She felt Patrick lay her down in a bed of hay and drape two blankets over her. He helped her out of her soaking wet gloves and footwear, before tucking the blankets in around her, and she wished she could wake up enough to thank him. Then she felt the comforting bulk of Simcoe laying down beside her and resting her head on Gemma's chest. There was the sound of wood crackling, matches scraping, a blaze catching flame and Patrick thanking God as he coaxed the fire to life. Slowly, she felt a tingle of warmth beginning to fill her body again.

"There we go," Patrick said. "That should help. Now all we've got to do is sit tight until the phone lines are up again and be sure not to panic."

What had Patrick said on the boat? Panicking didn't help anything.

She heard a deep, slow and sad sigh leave his chest. She couldn't begin to imagine the pain he must be feeling, knowing that his only child had been kidnapped and that he was helpless to find him. He had to be almost every bit as freezing cold and wet as she was, and yet his primary focus was taking care of her. Tears built underneath her lids. She heard him move across the floor toward her, then she felt him kneel down.

"Now," Patrick said, "I need you to open your eyes and wake up for me, okay?"

She tried to open her eyes. But somehow they stayed stubbornly closed. It was like she was locked—frozen—inside her own body and couldn't get out.

He reached for her hands, enveloped them inside of his.

"I'll tell you a secret," he went on. Gently, he rubbed his fingers along hers, massaging warmth back into them. "I think you're the smartest person I've ever met. Right now, I could really use you to help me think through how we're going to get out of this situation. So, I need you to wake up and activate that PI brain of yours. Because I'm counting on you to help me get out of here, get help and find my son."

He blew out a hard breath and then she heard him whisper. "Help me, Lord. I can't even tell if she's still breathing."

Her chest tightened as her own heart echoed his desperate prayer. Hot pins and needles danced over the surface of her skin. She willed herself to open her eyes and tried to force herself to sit up.

The floorboard creaked again. She felt him lean toward her. The warmth of his breath brushed against her skin. She could sense his mouth hovering over her face.

Seemed he was checking her breath and maybe considering CPR. Either way, his lips were now barely inches away from hers. His hand brushed tenderly along her neck, tilting her head back. Then his fingers cradled the back of her head. His face moved closer—

She tried again, this time jolting her body upright so suddenly that as she sat up, she bumped face first into Patrick. Her nose smashed painfully into his and their lips accidentally met.

Patrick jerked back on his heels, nearly falling backward in the darkened barn. Whether from the cold in his bones that was just beginning to thaw or her nearness, his heart was beating with a steady *rat-a-tat-tat*, like a timpani drum.

As for the tingling on his lips, he hadn't kissed someone since Lucy.

"I'm so sorry," he said, his voice almost choking on an embarrassed chuckle. "That was an accident. I was just checking you to see if you were breathing."

"I'm fine." Gemma sat up higher now. Her voice sounded a bit groggy still, but her blue eyes were wide and dazzling in the flickering firelight. She pushed the blankets down on top of Simcoe and waved both hands in front of her, as if trying to shove aside any uncomfortable or inconvenient thoughts the accidental moment might've raised between them. "It's okay... I know, you didn't mean... I didn't mean..."

Her voice trailed off and her head shook as if her mind had run out of possible words to finish the sentence.

"I know," he said, quickly, as if to reassure her that they were both on the same befuddled page.

Their lips had touched and neither of them knew what to say about it.

Gemma looked around, taking her surroundings in for the first time, and he followed her gaze.

The barn was large and mostly empty, except for a few old tools and electronics that looked like they'd been left on a paint-splattered tool bench sometime in the eighties. Rolls of old chicken wire fencing and siding board were stacked against one wall. A single closed door lay at one end of the barn. A large sliding double door lay toward the lake. He'd found it open and only managed to close it partway, showing a black sky and swirling snow beyond. A fire still blazed in the makeshift fireplace he'd built on a large concrete slab that looked like it had once held some kind of portable stove. Simcoe was still under the blankets, and judging by the kelpie's contended sigh, she was quite happy to stay there for now.

For Patrick, they could've been in a five-star hotel and every breath he had to wait before finding and saving Tristan would've still hurt so much it was agony. Once again, he tried to shove the pain away and clenched his jaw to keep the frustrated tears he felt building at the back of his eyes from falling.

They would find Tristan. He set his heart on the hope and faith it would happen.

And he would hold it together until then.

"Any idea where we are?" Patrick asked.

"No." Gemma frowned. "I don't recognize it. But there are a smattering of empty and abandoned buildings around the lake. How did you find it?"

"I just moved the boat as close as I could to the shore," he said, "and started scanning for a building. This is the first one I saw. I did look around outside for a second after setting you down, but I didn't see a home or any other buildings nearby."

Gemma pushed herself to sit even higher, until the blanket and dog were now just on her legs. Her fingers twitched and danced in the air in front of her, as if she was subconsciously searching for a missing computer keyboard.

"There might not be any other buildings," she said. "I'm just really thankful you found it."

"Me too," he said.

"Thank you for rescuing me."

"No worries." Despite the pain in his chest, he felt a faint smile cross his face. "It only seemed fair considering you rescued me from the men in fedoras."

The same men he could only assume had his son now.

"Technically, you've saved me twice now," Gemma said.

"Simcoe was the one who found you in the woods," he said. "I just helped."

A small laugh slipped through her lips. It was tinged with sadness and worry, yet it was also a spontaneous and beautiful sound. Then he watched her forehead line in worry.

"I'm so sorry that it's going to take us even longer to find Tristan," she said, "and let the authorities know he's been kidnapped. I'm guessing we still don't have a phone signal."

"No," he said.

"What happened to the men who were following us?" she asked.

"I haven't seen or heard a thing from them since we hit

the rock and you went overboard. I cut the engine then, and I think they couldn't see or hear us anymore."

She nodded as if taking the information in. "Well, thankfully it should be pretty hard for them to find us now."

"Yeah, I hope so."

But for now, all they could do was wait. Patrick turned back to the fire, pushed the burning branches around with the fire poker and added a new one, thankful there'd been so much usable wood in the barn.

"I wish I'd gotten a better look at the person who took Tristan," he admitted. "I assume it was Rust, as he was the only hostile who wasn't accounted for. But then, we still don't know why someone was writing to me pretending to be Tristan's mom and I still can't imagine why my son apparently climbed out the window before he was kidnapped."

Gemma didn't answer for a long moment. She was looking down and frowning, like she was lost in a bad mental prison that she couldn't escape from.

"Are you doing okay?" he asked.

Her lower lip quivered and then she shrugged. "I'm so sorry, I froze back there. Maybe if I hadn't, we'd be in a better place right now."

"Well, it's freezing cold out—"

"No." She looked up and met his eyes. "I mean my body just froze at the wheel when the men in fedoras were shooting at us. I shut down. It's like I couldn't move or even think."

Yeah, he'd noticed. But he hadn't been quite sure what to say about it. He checked that the life jacket had dried, then set it down on the floor opposite her and sat, cross-legged, with his knees just a few inches from her legs. The fire crackled and the wind blew, as he waited for her to say more. But although her lips moved, it was like she couldn't figure out what to say.

"Did something similar happen in the car after you rescued me after the crash?" he asked, gently.

"Yeah," she said. "It's the sound of gunshots that do it. Sometimes the sound of fireworks or when cars backfire close to me. It's like I get stuck back in the memory of the very first time someone fired a gun at me."

"I'm happy to listen if you want to talk about it," Patrick said.

Simcoe slid out from under the blankets, walked over to the fire and then sniffed it before lying down. Gemma pulled her knees up into her chest and wrapped her arms around them.

"Back when I was a solo PI, working alone and tracking my first serial killer, I thought I could take him on alone, with no backup. I was resentful back then, didn't even tell my brother—who's a cop—what I was doing, let alone ask him for help. When the killer hunted me down, he ran my car off the road into the river and fired his gun at me while it sank. He thought I drowned, and I nearly did."

"I'm so sorry." He reached his hand out into the space between them, wanting to comfort her and take away the pain he could see echoing in her eyes. But then the memory of that accidental kiss filled his mind, and he caught himself, pulled back, then crossed his arms in front of his chest. Thankfully, she didn't seem to notice. "That must've been terrifying."

"It was." Gemma nodded. "My brother thought I was dead too." What looked like regret filled her eyes. "Even though Jackson has become one of my best friends since that happened, a year and a half ago, it wasn't always that way," she said. "We were very different growing up, and for some reason it was like we were always at odds, even though we loved each other. When he started getting in trouble with the law, I was so angry at the way I saw the system treating him, it fueled my interest in becoming a private investigator. Then it was fueled even more when a friend of mine vanished in college, and the police didn't seem interested in finding her." Her shoulders rose and fell slowly. No wonder she was so motivated to bridge the gap between the police and potential witnesses who didn't want to talk to the police. "When Jackson went and became a cop it felt like he chose the wrong side."

"But you work with police now," Patrick pointed out.

"I do," Gemma said. Something wistful moved in her eyes as she looked past him and out at the blowing snow. "My team is amazing, and I wouldn't give them up for anything in the world."

She ran her hands over Simcoe's fur, as if grounding herself.

"Remember how I said that with criminals like the Noëlville Serial Killer it's all about creating fear?" she asked. "Well, in that moment when I was being shot at, it was like fear was a disease that took over me. But the worst part is what I did because of it. I hid off the grid for two weeks, letting my brother, my best friend and the people who cared about me think I was dead. Because it's like when I heard those gunshots being fired at me, and realized somebody was trying to murder me right there on the road, my brain got stuck in this stupid self-survival mode that made me want to push everybody away. That's the thing I can't get over. It felt like the right choice at the time, but looking back I wish I could just grab myself by the shoulders and shake some sense into me."

"Have you ever told Jackson that?" Patrick asked.

"I don't know," she said. "I think so. I have no doubt he's forgiven me."

"But, have you forgiven yourself for disappearing like that?"

Gemma tilted her head to the side and paused a long moment before answering. "No, I don't think I have."

"Well, it's a lot easier said than done." Patrick turned toward the fire and stretched out his legs. The snow had already erased any sign of their footprints from where they'd entered the barn. "Sometimes, I feel that the hardest person to forgive is yourself or to accept that God forgives you. I have never forgiven myself for the fact Lucy left us. Nor for Drew's betrayal." His chest tightened thinking of the man he knew as a killer. "And now, no matter how hard I pray and hope that Tristan is found save and alive, I don't think I'm ever going to forgive myself for the fact he was kidnapped."

"That wasn't your fault," Gemma said.

He didn't turn.

"My son pilfered a pair of sneakers and hopefully some kind of jacket out of your cottage cupboard," he said, "and snuck out of a second-story window to meet someone without me knowing—and they kidnapped him." The desperate ache that he'd felt in his chest ever since he'd looked out the window to see his son being taken at gunpoint grew sharper. "What if he thought it was Lucy? You said you saw a woman outside the diner. What if he snuck out of the diner to meet someone he thought was his mother and then when Rust's gunshot scared her off, she tried again at the cottage? I never talked to him about Lucy, and I changed the subject whenever he brought it up. I felt too ashamed of the kind of person she'd been, the kind of life she'd led and how our relationship had ended. So, he didn't grow up with a sense of who his mother was, and that's my fault. I didn't tell him that Lucy was dead at the hands of the Noëlville Serial Killer. I also never told him about the letters and gifts for him that I've been getting from somebody pretending to be his mom. What if the person who reached out to me pretending to be Lucy reached out to him as well? What if he felt like he couldn't talk to me about her and like he had to sneak around behind my back to have any kind of relationship with her? What if it's my fault he didn't trust me?"

"It's possible," Gemma said, softly. "I wish I could tell you it wasn't, but you also said that you needed to focus on facts right now."

Yeah, he had. Although he hadn't realized that she'd heard him say it.

"But I also don't think that drowning yourself in hypothetical blame over something that could have happened if you'd done something differently is going to help you," she went on. "It's possible you could've done everything right and he'd have still been kidnapped. Fact is, we don't know how the Noëlville Serial Killer plays into this, or Rust, Umber and Bone either. There are too many pieces on the board right now. Three men in fedoras, a serial killer, a mom-imposter, a theft, and I don't have any idea how they all fit together."

"Is it possible that either Rust, Umber or Bone is the one who reached out to me pretending to be Lucy and that one of them kidnapped Tristan?" Patrick asked. "I didn't get a good look at the kidnapper."

"Maybe the woman I saw at the diner is an innocent bystander who had nothing to do with this?" Gemma mused. "Or maybe she's Missy/Marissa who has also been pretending to be Lucy. Either way, why did Tristan climb out the window? Is she the kidnapper?"

"How did anyone even track Tristan to the cottage?" Patrick asked. "Did she and/or the men in fedoras also track us to the diner?"

"I don't know anything for sure," Gemma started, then added, "Not yet anyway. I'm itching to get my hands on a computer and phone. But I have a theory. You said that Tristan bought his LMNTL game console off a friend. Yet, those devices are really pricey, and as I mentioned they have chat capability. What if the person who's been pretending to be Lucy somehow sent it to him—"

"And he lied to me because he knew I'd have taken it away from him," Patrick added. Yeah, as much as he hated to admit it, that was definitely possible. Especially now that he knew Tristan was capable of sneaking around behind his back. "He loves that console more than anything."

"It's also possible that whoever gave it to him put an electronic tracking device in it," Gemma said.

Patrick leaped to his feet. "I brought it with me!"

"You brought it with you?" Gemma repeated.

"Yes!" He ran for the rucksack. "I thought it would comfort Tristan to have it when we found him."

It had never crossed his mind that the men in fedoras could use it to track them now!

He reached into the bag and yanked it out.

"It's not charged though," he said, "can it still emit a signal?"

"Yes. Because the transmitter might not be connected to the main battery."

Which meant, someone could be using it to track him now. He dropped it on the floor and raised his foot to stomp it into smithereens.

"No, wait, stop!" Gemma stood and grabbed his arm. "We need to check the chat messages once it's charged and see if there's any data on it we can use to track whoever took him. Our fake-Lucy may have been using it to communicate with him. For now, we can just build a Faraday cage to disable the signal."

"What's that?" He stepped back quickly as Gemma darted

forward, scooped the LMNTL console off the floor and yanked out the batteries. "What are you talking about?"

But she was already running for the chicken wire in the corner of the room and lifting it onto the tool bench.

"It's like a cocoon that shields electronic devices and blocks electromagnetic fields and radio waves," she called. "You can build them out of wire mesh. Grab the rucksack and come help me. We need to cut and bend this wire, and I'm not strong enough to do it on my own without some much better tools."

He understood what she was saying—in fact he vaguely remembered hearing of a Faraday cage on a science fiction television show—but he wasn't sure how much he believed it was possible to construct such a contraption out of chicken wire in a run-down barn. Still, he cut the wire as she instructed and helped her bend it around the LMNTL over and over again, folding it in at the edges, until the game console looked well and truly caged.

Would it actually work?

"Now we just need some kind of bag to put it in to hold it all together," Gemma said, "since unfortunately I don't have a soldering iron. I only grabbed a mini-roll of duct tape, and I don't want to use it all on this." Her lips pursed in thought. "How far away is the boat? There's a sealable waterproof bag in the glove compartment. That might work."

"It's not that far," Patrick said. "I can run for it and be back in five. You stay here, with Simcoe. Hold on to the axe and yell for me if you hear so much as a twig break outside."

"Will do." Gemma smiled mildly. "I'm sure I'll be fine."

He turned away and dashed out into the snow again. This time, despite the furious wind that whipped around him and the snow up to his shins, it was almost a relief to be out of the warm barn and back in the storm again.

There'd been something too cozy about being in the barn with Gemma, beyond just the fire he'd managed to build. His face grew hot when he looked at her, the back of his neck burned at the sound of her voice. He needed to feel the sting of the cold.

Being around Gemma impacted him in a way that unsettled him.

The inconvenient fact of the matter was that he was attracted to her, in a way that he hadn't been drawn to anyone in years—maybe even ever. She was remarkably pretty, incredibly smart, not to mention unbelievably compassionate and understanding. But the very last thing he could do right now was allow himself to feel any kind of feelings for anybody. If he couldn't trust his own heart or his judgment, how could he begin to try and build a relationship with someone? Let alone for a woman who was committed to living in the big city, over five hours' drive from the home and business he'd built on Manitoulin Island and hoped to pass on to Tristan as his inheritance.

His son's optimistic and cheerful face filled his mind, and suddenly the aching pain in Patrick's chest sharpened so fiercely that he clutched it and wondered if this was what an actual heart attack felt like.

His son was in danger and needed him to focus his full attention on finding him. If Patrick hadn't let himself be distracted by a private conversation with Gemma back at the cottage, would Tristan have been able to sneak out of the house without him noticing?

Help me, Lord! I feel lost in more ways than one. How can two sets of conflicting emotions exist in my heart without tearing me to pieces?

No, he wouldn't—he couldn't—let himself fall for Gemma. His son's life and future depended on it.

He found the boat where he'd left it, wedged between the rocks and anchored by the snow. Getting in and out was a bit trickier now due to the fresh build-up of ice and snow. But within a few freezing moments, he found the waterproof bag, stuffed it inside his pocket and started back for the barn. They were down to one flashlight now since the other one had died when he'd gone through the ice after Gemma, and while they had phones, there was no way to charge them without electricity. So, he switched the flashlight off, zipped it up inside his coat and let himself be guided back to the barn by the orange glow of the firelight he could see flickering through the open door.

Partick was a couple of yards away when he heard the sound of footsteps running quickly toward him through the snow. Quickly, he stepped behind a tree, froze and listened. At first, it sounded like some kind of large four-legged animal. A coyote or a wolf perhaps seeking shelter from the storm in the barn where Gemma and Simcoe were now hiding? But then he saw a dark silhouette move across the beam of light that cascaded down the hill.

No, not an animal. It was a man. He was tall with broad shoulders and the unmistakable outline of a gun in his hand. Slowly and cautiously, the figure moved toward the open barn.

One of the criminals had found them. And he was going to kill Gemma if Patrick didn't find a way to stop him.

SEVEN

Something roared to life inside Patrick's core just as suddenly and powerfully as if an engine had ignited inside him. No, he wasn't about to let this stranger hurt Gemma. Not on his watch.

Patrick dashed through the trees, his feet churning up the snow as he sprinted through the storm toward the stranger. The gunman was bearded and wore a thick winter tuque and jacket. So, not Rust, Umber or Bone then. But that didn't mean he was safe. The figure paused and looked around, as if he could hear Patrick coming but wasn't able to figure out where he was. Patrick was going to make sure he didn't get the opportunity. The gunman might have a weapon, but Patrick had the element of surprise and was going to use it for all he was worth.

He leaped out of the trees and threw himself full force at the gunman. Gemma shouted something in the distance, but he couldn't make out the words. Patrick caught the man around the waist in a football tackle and brought him to the ground. But it was a short-lived victory. The bearded man reared back. His elbow caught the side of Patrick's head in a punishing blow. Patrick hit the ground and rolled, as the sound of his own jaw cracking filled his ears. A deep growl moved from somewhere in the shadows.

The gunman scrambled up and aimed his weapon down at Patrick's form. "Stay down! I'm here for Gemma."

But Patrick wasn't about to listen. Instead, he leaped up and squared off against the man. His hands balled into fists. "If you want to get to her, you're going to have to go through me first!"

"Is that so?" the gunman asked, in a curious tone that Patrick couldn't quite place. He lowered the gun.

"Jackson! Patrick!" Gemma shouted. "We're all on the same side."

Jackson? This gunman was Gemma's brother, K-9 Officer Jackson Locke? Patrick glanced toward the open door and saw Gemma standing there, flanked by two majestic dogs. She had one hand on Simcoe's collar and the other on a German shepherd.

Gemma sighed, turning to her brother. "I have a lot to explain and a lot of questions about how you found me. But sadly, we don't have time for any of this. Patrick's son Tristan was kidnapped, and we need to contact the police and put out an Amber Alert immediately. Can you get us out of here?"

"No," Jackson's tone shifted immediately. Suddenly he was serious and all business. He turned to Patrick. "Long story short, but we're snowed in for now."

"How about a phone connection?" Patrick asked.

"I'm sorry," Jackson said, "the roads and phone lines are down over a huge radius. All I have is my radio, and it's only got a range of a few miles. But the good news is, on the drive up I discovered a network of old-timers, law enforcement and first responders have been using the shortwave radios to check in on each other and look out for people the best they can. Hopefully, one way or the other we'll be able to reach somebody who's able to reach someone with a working phone."

They stepped into the barn entrance, and Jackson immediately started trying to find an open radio channel. They'd put all other talk on hold for now. For a long and agonizing moment, all they could hear was static, as he tried channel after channel, in hopes of finding anyone who'd answer. Finally, they manage to reach a retired cop, who said he'd radio his brother, who'd then brave the storm to reach his nephew, who was a paramedic, had a working 911 connection and could be counted on to make sure word got out about Tristan's abduction.

"Don't worry." Jackson brushed a hand on Patrick's shoulder and then put the radio way. "The information is going to get passed along and shared, until by the time the power comes back across the province tomorrow everyone will be on the lookout for your son. Don't underestimate the power of teamwork."

"I'll try not to." Patrick exhaled slowly, and tried to keep his calm. Despite the glimmer of hope that Jackson's arrival had brought, they still weren't out of the woods yet. "Thanks again."

"No problem."

They did their best to close the door as far as it would go. Then Patrick, Gemma and Jackson sat around the fire—Gemma on the blanket, Patrick on the life jacket and Jackson on a block of wood—while Simcoe and Hudson curled up together as close as they could safely get to the makeshift firepit.

"You sure you can't evacuate us to some better, well-lit and secure location with a working internet connection," Gemma asked, ruefully.

"Yeah, sadly I wasn't joking about the roads being closed." Jackson ran his hand over his beard. "I was already in the truck and heading up here within half an hour of Caleb telling me that Patrick had been kidnapped, once I made sure that Blake was able to take Amy and Skye to her place and keep an eye on them. The drive took me hours longer than it should have, I lost cell phone service two hours ago, and quite frankly if it wasn't for four-wheel drive I'd have been stuck under a snowbank ages ago."

"I don't know whether to thank you for coming after me," Gemma said, "or give you grief for being foolish enough to drive through a storm to do it."

"I prefer to think of it as determined," her brother said. "Besides, I know you'd do the same for me."

Patrick enjoyed seeing the genuine affection between the siblings, especially considering what Gemma had told him about their past.

Then Jackson glanced around the barn. "Considering what it's like out there and how long it's been since I've seen anyone with power, I think our wisest course of action is to camp out here overnight and make our way back to civilization when the snow stops and the sun rises. I've got a bunch of camping supplies in my truck, and there are much worse places than this to be stuck. I don't think we're going to find a much better option."

Patrick sighed. Not the answer he was hoping for, but he'd also weathered enough bad Canadian storms to trust that what the cop was saying was most likely true. People froze to death on the side of the road when a blizzard got this bad. At least here they had shelter and heat.

Gemma filled Jackson in on the details of Rust, Bone and Umber and the events of the night, along with their theories so far about Lucy and her death. She leaned forward, and her hands punctuated the air as she gave a very direct, concise and focused briefing that hit all the important points without getting sidetracked. Patrick was impressed.

Gold and brown shadows danced down the beautiful lines of her face, as the flames flickered before her. When Gemma was done, she took a big breath and let it out slowly. "So, is the cottage still standing? Or was it burned down because I led multiple criminals directly to it? I've been afraid to ask."

"Oh, it's still there," Jackson said and sighed. "That's the good news. But yeah, sadly it was tossed, I'm guessing by your three men in brown hats. Somebody broke through the big picture window and ransacked the place a bit. It'll be a clean-up job and it'll probably be a few days before we can move back in, not that the cottage has power anyway. But the place is still standing. It was clear they were looking for something. But I didn't notice anything stolen or even broken, besides the window. I think it's pretty clear they weren't interested in robbing the place, so much as looking for something."

"The stolen stash," Patrick said. "Whatever that is."

"How did they search it?" Gemma asked. "Was it small-scale or large-scale? Drawers or doors?"

Jackson paused and his eyes closed, like he was mentally going from room to room, trying to recreate the scene in his mind.

Patrick felt his forehead wrinkle. "What do you mean?"

Gemma turned toward him.

"If they yanked out all the drawers and dumped the cutlery on the floor, then they're looking for something small," Gemma said, "like a thumb drive or envelope. Which could mean the stash is incriminating information about someone important."

"Like the Noëlville Serial Killer," Jackson interjected, with his eyes still closed.

"Really?" Gemma turned to him. "You think the Noëlville Serial Killer is somebody powerful enough to hire three armed goons to chase down a thumb drive of incriminating information on him?"

"No, I don't think most serial killers have private security in eight-hundred-dollar hats." Jackson opened his eyes. "But I seem to remember you saying once that there are no bad ideas in a brainstorm. In answer to your question, it was a large-scale search. If I were to guess, they were looking for something big. Like a safe…or maybe a corpse."

A shudder ran through Patrick's inner core and he found himself praying for the millionth time that his son was okay.

"So maybe the stash is a dead body." Gemma's shoulder shook as if a shiver had just run up her spine. "Must admit I hadn't even considered that. And unfortunately, it's going to be a while before I can actually research anything, run those men's faces or even hope to get answers. I came up here with one clear and simple goal—to pursue the case of the Noëlville Serial Killer who killed seven people, including Lucy, and left their bodies wrapped in plastic. Now Tristan's gone, three strangers are after us, we're drowning in questions and we've got nothing."

"Well, at least we've still got your brain," Patrick said, "and it seems to be doing pretty well for us, at least from where I'm sitting."

"Thanks," Gemma said. "Your brain's pretty impressive too." She gave him a smile that seemed to quirk just slightly higher on one side than the other. And Patrick felt a half a smile tugging at the corner of his lips in return. Then the floorboards creaked behind him as Jackson shifted his perch on the block of wood he'd chosen for a seat. And when Patrick looked his way, the cop had a curious look on his face.

"Anyway," Gemma said, quickly. "You never explained how you found us."

"That was all him." Jackson pointed to the German shepherd now snoring in front of the fire. "There's a reason Finnick calls him the best search and rescue dog he's ever met. When we got to the cottage and found it empty, Hudson tracked your scent to the boathouse, so I knew you were somewhere around the lake. So, I drove around the lake really slowly with the window open, and Hudson stuck his head out and kept sniffing for you. Whenever we hit a juncture, I let him out and he sniffed the ground. He really is an amazing dog."

Jackson reached down and scratched his partner behind the ears. Then he stood. "I'm going to head back to my truck and grab my gear before the weather gets any worse. Then we can set up for the night. I suggest we take turns sleeping with one person on lookout at all times. Not that the dogs won't warn us if they hear someone coming." He glanced at Patrick. "Mind coming with me and giving me a hand?"

"Sure," Patrick said. A moment later, he was heading back out in the snow again, this time following Hudson as the dog led them back toward the truck. "I'm sorry for jumping you like that."

"No problem," Jackson said, and while Patrick couldn't see his face, but there was an odd, almost worried tone in his voice that he couldn't quite place. "I'm really glad to know you have my sister's back." He paused and their feet crunched in the snow for another long moment. "I knew she was touching base with you about the Noëlville Serial Killer and that you'd met her with the rest of the team last Christmas, but I didn't realize you two were so...close."

"Close?" Patrick choked as hard as if Jackson had just physically slapped him on the back. "We're not. I mean, your sister is a really wonderful human being, but..."

But what? His words spluttered out. He'd been about to point out they barely knew each other. Yet, somehow that no longer rang true. It was like he'd been so focused on his fear and drive to find Tristan, he somehow hadn't realized just how much his heart has been slowly creeping closer to the tenacious PI who'd been helping him.

Jackson didn't answer and Patrick couldn't find any more words to say. So, instead, the men just kept walking, each lost in their own thoughts. Finally, the outline of the truck appeared in the glow of Jackson's flashlight. It was already buried under several inches of snow. When they reached it, they stopped. Jackson turned toward him, and Patrick could see the concern etched on Gemma's brother's face.

"I promise you that we are going to do everything in our power to find your son," Jackson said. "You can count on that. We won't rest until he's found."

"Thank you," Patrick said and he meant it, but he was also unsettled to see how worried Jackson looked.

"I just wanted to warn you," Jackson said. "My sister doesn't trust a lot of people. She finds it hard to even open up to me. I saw how she looks at you, and quite frankly, the way you look at her back. Just be careful, okay?"

Patrick stepped back. "I'm not going to hurt your sister. I don't even know what you're talking about—"

Jackson held up his hand. "In my experience," he cut him off, "getting close to someone you're working on a case with is like playing with matches. Everybody needs to be at the top of their game if we're going to find your son. I'm not going to tell you how to manage your personal business, and I know Gemma far too well to try to interfere with hers. I'm just telling you to tread carefully, because once a fire starts burning there's no way of knowing what will go up in flames."

Gemma didn't expect she'd be able to sleep that night, despite the aching fatigue that coursed through her limbs. But when the men and Hudson got back from the truck, it turned out that her brother had a small cocoon-style tent, which would allow her an extra level of privacy within the barn. When she crawled inside, tucked herself into one of Jackson's below-zero sleeping bags and felt Simcoe curl up inside there with her, she fell asleep almost immediately. Then she opened her eyes to see bright sunshine streaming through the orange walls of the tent. She stretched, rolled over and realized that Simcoe had slipped out of a gap in the zipper sometime in the night.

Silence fell outside the tent, punctuated only by the light rustling of tree branches and the faint sound of water lapping against the icy rocks. She let out a long, deep breath and prayed.

Lord, give me the strength and wisdom I need to face today. Keep Tristan safe and help us find him, please. We need Your guidance and Your help. I can't do this without You.

There'd been an odd, awkward and uncomfortable silence between Jackson and Patrick when they'd returned, as if they'd had a conversation when they were out in the snow that neither of them wanted to fill her in on. She'd have tried to pry into it, but Patrick stepped outside almost immediately to keep the first watch. She fished her phone from her pocket and turned it on. It was just past seven thirty in the morning on Christmas Eve. She still had absolutely no signal. Not even the flicker of a bar.

Finnick was getting married later tonight in a candlelight wedding. Thankfully he was already on the island preparing for the wedding. She wondered when the roads would open and how many of the guests would be able to brave the snow to make it there—including her, Patrick and her colleagues on the task force.

Gemma lay there for a moment, prayed, and felt a Bible

verse from Philippians 4 fill her thoughts. *And the peace of God, which passeth all understanding, shall keep your hearts and minds through Christ Jesus.*

Then she unzipped her sleeping bag, crawled out into the barn and stood up. Through a gap in the barn door, she saw Patrick sitting on a log a few feet away, watching as the sun climbed higher above the lake. She put her coat and boots on and stepped outside, and then saw that Simcoe was sitting tall beside Patrick. The K-9's huge pointed ears twitched as Gemma approached. Simcoe's tail wagged hard, kicking up the snow. Patrick turned. For the second time in twenty-four hours she was shocked by just how much her heart fluttered when their eyes met, and suddenly the memory of their completely accidental kiss the night before filled her mind.

She took a deep breath and pushed the thought away.

"Good morning," she called. "Merry Christmas Eve."

"Hey." A tired smile crossed his handsome face.

"What's new?"

"Nothing much," Patrick said. "Snow stopped. Phones are still dead. Jackson has gone to dig out the truck. We figured we'd give you until seven-thirty and then try to get the vehicle back on the road." He brushed the snow off the log beside him. "Have a seat."

She crossed the ground toward him, carefully stepping in the footprints he'd left to keep from sinking too deeply into the snow. She sat down. Simcoe walked over and lay down on Gemma's feet, and she ran her hand over the dog's fur.

"How are you doing?" she asked.

"I'm alright," Patrick said. "More worried for my son than I've ever been in my life, but I actually managed to sleep a couple of hours, which is good."

"It is," she said. "I've laid awake praying a bit too and thinking about Philippians 4."

"The peace which surpasses understanding." Patrick pulled a metal thermos out of the snow beside him and handed it to her. "Here, try this."

She undid the top and the scent of something chocolatey and mint filled her senses. Then she took a sip. It was delicious and tasted like Christmas. "It's amazing. What is it?"

"Lake water, heated over the fire, combined with a packet of instant coffee and a handful of peppermint chocolates I got from the diner. Help yourself. I've had plenty."

She took another long sip. For a long moment, neither of them said anything, and for the first time that morning Gemma looked around and took in the day.

Blue skies stretched out endlessly above, punctuated only by the bright sun that beat down around them and warmed her face. About two feet of snow cast a thick white blanket on the ground and hung heavy on the trees. The lake was a pale bluish gray, punctuated by snow-covered rocks and islands. She couldn't see either her cottage or the town of Cedar Lake from here, but finally she had a sense of where on the lake they were.

"I honestly can't tell if the snow was higher when I was a kid, or if I was just shorter," Patrick said. When he turned toward her, the dazzling sun seemed to cast golden flecks dancing in his eyes, and something turned serious in his gaze. "How could you possibly choose to live in the big city after living somewhere like this?"

"I love my work," she admitted. "It doesn't feel like a job. It feels like a calling. I get to help solve murders, stop criminals and change lives."

Patrick nodded slowly, like he was understanding more than she was saying.

"And you can't do that from the middle of nowhere," he said.

"No, I can't," she said. "You can't do the kind of research I do without the phone and reliable, high-speed internet. But also, because I need to coordinate with local, provincial and federal law enforcement, not to mention interviewing witnesses."

Again, Patrick nodded slowly, and they lapsed back into a silence that didn't feel quite as comfortable as before. Then Patrick sighed.

She grabbed his hands, wanting to offer him comfort. He must be so anxious about his son.

"I have a friend named Teresa who has a cottage on this lake," she said, "she counsels a lot of kids who've dealt with hard things. Maybe when we find Tristan and get him home safely, it might help for you guys to talk with her a bit."

Patrick swallowed hard. "Thank you. That's a great idea. I just can't stop feeling like I've failed him."

She squeezed his hands reassuringly. He squeezed her fingers back, and neither of them pulled away.

"I think you're amazing," she said honestly. He'd kept calm even in this nightmare. "I can't imagine the pain and fear that you've been going through. But I want you to know that I'm here for you, not just as a member of the Cold Case Task Force, but also as a friend."

He chuckled softly. "Thank you. I think you're amazing too."

Warmth bloomed in her chest. "And despite how terrifying and horrible yesterday was, I can't help but thank God that you were the person who was beside me through all that. You weren't only quick thinking enough to save both our lives in a pinch, you stayed calm too, and you helped redirect my mind on the stuff that really mattered. I'm just glad that if I had to be in a foxhole like that, you were the one I was in that foxhole with."

"Yeah," Gemma said. "I feel the same way about going through all that with you too."

Then, in a movement as instinctive and natural as breathing, she found herself pulling her hands away from his and wrapping them around his neck, just as he opened his arms and pulled her into his chest. And in that moment, she had no idea whether she was the one who hugged him first or whether he was the one who reached for her. All she knew was that she was hugging Patrick Craft in a way that somehow felt safer and more comfortable than any hug she'd ever experienced before.

The hug lingered. Then, instead of pulling away, she let her head fall into the crook of his neck and lean against his chest until she could hear the steady beat of his pulse. Slowly, Patrick raised one hand and ran it along the back of her head, gently curling it through the hair at the nape of her neck before letting it slide down her back again. Still, neither of them pulled away. Gemma tilted her face up. Their eyes met. And she felt his warm breath on her skin.

Suddenly a loud and annoying electronic siren noise seemed to blare from all directions at once. She leaped to her feet and so did Patrick.

It was an Amber Alert!

"Tristan!"

They shouted the boy's name at the same time, their voices overlapping as they both reached for their phones. There it was in a big orange bar at the top of their screens.

It was an Amber Alert for Tristan Craft.

Tears flooded Gemma's eyes, and she didn't even try to wipe them away, as she read the words on the screen, praying that someone would see them, know something and answer.

Then her phone began to chime with dozens and dozens of message alerts cascading down her screen. Jackson ran out of the woods with his phone in his hand, Hudson by his side and his hair standing up in all directions, looking like he'd just leaped straight to his feet out of a dead sleep. Patrick seemed to be checking his voicemail. Then before any of them could dial, she watched as the color drained from his face. He grabbed her shoulder with one hand and pushed the phone up to her ear with the other.

"You have one new message," an electronic female voice said.

Then a scared and young voice filled the line.

"Dad? It's me, Tristan. I'm safe and I'm okay. I'm so sorry, I just wanted to meet Mom. She says she needs one of the presents she sent me, and wants me to—"

There was a bang, a long beep and then the line when dead.

EIGHT

For a moment, so many different emotions crashed over Patrick at the sound of his son's voice that he felt immobilized under the weight of them all. He was vaguely aware of Gemma and Jackson saying something, but the world outside the phone in his hand suddenly felt muted and far away.

Immediately, Patrick opened the call log, spotted the unknown number his son had called him from and hit redial.

It rang over and over and over again. Then finally, someone answered.

"Hello?" The voice was male, hesitant and one Patrick didn't ever remember hearing before.

"Hi, I'm Patrick and my son Tristan called from this number."

Silence fell on the other end.

Please Lord, don't let him hang up before I find out where my son is.

Suddenly he remembered what Gemma had told him back at the diner. *Sometimes the people who do have important information won't come forward because they don't want to get in trouble with the police, like former criminals. My role is to help get through to those people who don't trust the cops on my team and convince them that we're all in this together.*

"Please don't hang up," Patrick added, quickly. "I don't

want to get you or anybody in trouble. I'm just a worried dad looking for his son."

"There was an Amber Alert," the voice said. "It was all on the television and my phone. It woke me up."

"Yes," Patrick said, slowly, feeling like he was moving over thin ice. "So, you saw my Tristan?"

No response. He looked up and saw Gemma standing by his shoulder, with her eyes on his face. She nodded, smiled and waved her hand in a rolling motion.

Good job, she mouthed silently. *Keep going.*

"Thank you so much for letting him use your phone," Patrick said. "He sounded really scared, and I just want to know he's okay. Do you know where he is now?"

"Are you police?" The man countered Patrick's question with another one of his own. "Or with the police? I don't want to deal with cops."

There was the sound of footsteps retreating behind him. Patrick looked to see Jackson flashing him a thumbs-up and walking backward toward the barn, just far enough to give Patrick plausible deniability about a cop being there. Patrick waved a hand to him in thanks. Then he glanced at Gemma, who stayed rooted by his side.

"No, I'm not a cop and no police are listening in on this call," Patrick said. "I promise."

Another pause.

"I'm Patrick. What can I call you?"

"Gabe."

Gemma's fingers began to fly over her cell phone. It looked like she was searching up something in a browser. Then she held up the phone screen toward him. He read: Gabriel Rodriguez was Marissa Kerry's boyfriend, on and off for like 15 years.

Patrick nodded to show he'd understood. Then he took her phone and typed back.

The name Gabriel fits with her nickname for him being Angel.

But was this Gabriel about to help him find his son?

"Oh, hey!" Patrick said. His tone was upbeat and casual, but he felt like he was walking across a very thin sheet of ice again. "I used to be in a thing with Lucy a long time ago. She was close friends with your girl Marissa Kerry, right? Went by Missy?"

"Yeah," Gabe said, "but Missy's not in my life now or anything."

Well, that pretty much confirmed their suspicion about Missy being Marissa. Gemma was still typing furiously. She held up the phone again.

He and Missy both have records for theft. He can't have any contact with Missy as a condition of his parole or he'll go to jail.

"I get that," Patrick told Gabe. *Guide me, Lord.* "And again, I'm not here to cause Missy or anyone any trouble. I just want to make sure Tristan's okay. You know Lucy died, right? Tristan is her son."

Again, he focused on keeping his voice chill and nonthreatening, as if he was reconnecting with an acquaintance at a Christmas party. But it must've hit a nerve because Gabe sighed loudly like a broken diesel truck.

"Oh, don't worry, I know," Gabe said. He sounded frustrated. "I mean, it's not my place to set the kid straight. But I'm going to tell him anyway. Because I don't know what

Missy is playing at now by trying to pretend she's his mom. Maybe it's guilt over getting Lucy killed. But I think it's weird and it's sick. I only let her in because it was snowing and she had a kid with her. But when I told him the truth and snuck him my phone, she got mad and they left."

"What town are you in?" he asked. "When did they leave?"

"I don't know," he said. "She wants one of the gifts she sent him back—"

"She can have them—"

"But she wants him to help her with something first."

"Help her? With what?"

"I don't know. Look, your kid is alive and well. Missy won't hurt him. I gotta go."

"Wait!" Patrick said. "Do you know where she was taking him?"

"I don't know!" the man snapped. "But she said she wanted to take the kid to hit a place in Noëlville. Says it's the big one and then she's out of the life forever."

The call ended. Panic gripped him. Patrick called back and the number was blocked.

Still he tried over and over again, anxiety rising, until finally Gemma placed a hand on his. Only then did he stop and turn to her.

"What do we do?" he asked.

"We call my team."

Not ten minutes later, Simcoe and Hudson were back in their post by the fire, as Patrick, Jackson and Gemma sat uneasily in a circle, holding their phones in front of their faces and watching anxiously as one by one the members of the Cold Case Task Force joined the video call.

With the cottage ransacked and the roads impassable, a video call was the best they could do—though meeting in person at Gemma's cottage would have been ideal. The first to join the call was Officer Caleb Pine who immediately informed them he was busy figuring out which roads around Cedar Lake were navigable. He had a blond crew cut and the kind of jaw Patrick would've expected to see in a stock photo labeled "cop." Caleb also looked like he hadn't slept since he'd gotten off the phone with them the night before.

The second box contained a dark-haired officer who introduced herself as Sergeant Blake Murphy. She explained she was with the provincial police and coordinating with the task force on the Noëlville Serial Killer investigation. Beside her sat a pretty brunette who introduced herself as Jackson's wife, Amy, the artist. While they waited for the others, she quickly took descriptions of Rust, Bone and Umber, which she used to create composite sketches the team could use to search the men's faces through various databases, and then left the call.

Next came Officer Lucas Harper, a young cop with an impressive mustache and a golden Lab he introduced as his K-9 partner, Michigan. He was followed by a male officer with a deep voice who introduced himself only as Oscar and didn't turn his camera on.

"Alright," Gemma started to say, "I think we're all here and ready to go—"

But then, with a chiming sound, a final box opened on the screen, and Patrick looked to see his friend Inspector Ethan Finnick, head of the Cold Case Task Force. His retired K-9, Nippy, dozed behind him on the couch.

"Boss!" Gemma sat up straight. "What are you doing here? Aren't you getting married tonight?"

"I am." Finnick ran a hand over his graying beard. "Got a whole lot of shoveling to do to make sure everyone can make it safely to the ceremony tonight, not to mention helping Casey with a million last-minute details. But I heard you guys were in trouble and I couldn't sit this one out. It doesn't feel right to celebrate when Tristan's in trouble." He turned to Patrick. "I'm so sorry and I can only imagine what you're going through. He's an amazing kid and we're all going to do everything in our power to bring him home safely." The other officers chimed in, echoing Finnick's promise.

"Thank you," Patrick said. "I appreciate that."

Juniper Cove was a close-knit community and Finnick was one of the best men Patrick had ever met. While Finnick didn't come out and say he was going to cancel the wedding if Tristan wasn't found, Patrick wouldn't be surprised if they postponed. Silently, he prayed that it would not come to that.

Gemma briefed the team on everything that had happened with the Noëlville Serial Killer case, the attacks by Rust, Bone and Umber, and Tristan's abduction. He could see the looks of shock and surprise on their faces and caught more than a few gasps here and there. He hadn't realized just how much had changed about their investigation in the past few hours. Then again, the idea that Lucy had been killed by a serial killer and that this was somehow connected to his son's abduction would've felt pretty unbelievable if it wasn't for the constant fear that stabbed like a knife in his chest.

"I've already pulled the call records to trace Patrick's call with Gabriel," Caleb said. "I can confirm the phone belonged to a Gabriel Rodriguez, who was in a relationship with Marissa 'Missy' Kerry. Both have long criminal records for robbery and identity theft. The phone has been disconnected, but I've now got a warrant issued for Missy Kerry's arrest."

"And her name has been added to the Amber Alert," Blake added, "so now her face is plastered all over the news. She won't get far."

Patrick thanked God for that, then also worried it might

drive her and Tristan underground. Or cause her to do something dangerous and drastic.

"What frustrates me," Caleb said, "is that the original investigation was so badly bungled that, until we got our hands on it, nobody realized that the wallet found on the original victim belonged to someone who was still going around committing crimes."

"This might be a dumb question," Lucas said, "but why haven't we asked provincial police to go pick this Gabriel guy up for questioning?"

"It's not a bad question," Gemma said. "It's just a tricky situation. We don't know where he is, and I got the impression that he was telling us everything he knew. We have to weigh how much more he might know against the downside of losing his willingness to cooperate with us in the future. He's potentially facing five years in prison on larceny charges if a judge decides to revoke his probation for talking to Missy."

"So, I'm back-channeling a conversation with Gabe's public defender," Finnick added, "and trying to locate him and facilitate some agreement where he gets immunity if he provides information about Tristan's kidnapping, or anything pertaining to Missy or to Lucy's death. We want to encourage people to stick their necks out to help police find missing children. It'll take some time to cross all the *t*'s and dot all the *i*'s, but I'm hopeful."

"Gemma." Oscar's deep voice filled the line, and it was odd not to have a face to attach it to. "When Finnick called me in on this, his working theory was that there was no such thing as the Noëlville Serial Killer, but multiple killers using the same dumping ground in the forest between the small town of Noëlville and the city of Sudbury."

"Correct," Finnick chimed in. "My main question is still

whether they're unconnected killers or a team of killers working together."

"Less that twenty-four hours into your investigation of the first victim," Oscar went on, "Patrick's son has been kidnapped by an old friend of his late mother's, who happens to have a criminal record for petty theft. Plus, three well-paid men who you think might be private security have terrorized you, looking for some stash that somebody stole. Does that pretty much sum it up?"

"Yup, pretty much," Gemma said and nodded.

"Also," Patrick added, "I think Missy's been writing to me for weeks pretending to be Tristan's mother, and it looks like she convinced Tristan that she's his mom. I don't know why. But she sent him a lot of expensive gifts, including the LMNTL game console she used to contact him."

"Which is currently wrapped in chicken wire thanks to my sister's quick thinking," Jackson said, "and which we can hack into when we're back in civilization."

"What were the other gifts?" Oscar asked.

"Typical preteen boy stuff," Patrick said. "High end. Expensive sneakers, designer clothes, video games and a teen-sized punching bag for boxing. Apparently she wants one of them back. But I've opened them all. There's nothing suspicious there."

"And we can assume Missy isn't getting her hand on expensive swag like that in a legal way?" Caleb said, dryly.

"We'll definitely take another look at them," Finnick said. "Any of you got any thoughts about where we go next?"

"I'm thinking we've got all these different things going on, and I'm wondering what the connection is between them all," Oscar said, and Patrick had the feeling the unseen man was jabbing a finger at the air. "Is there a way all this connects?

Because my gut thinks there is. My gut tells me that none of this is coincidental. But brain's just not playing ball on that."

Heads nodded around the barn and on the screen.

The team moved on to reviewing what was known about the Noëlville Serial Killer's victims, starting with Lucy. As Jackson put it, "Maybe if we take a step back we'll see something we're missing."

Patrick hadn't heard of any of the other victims, and as the Cold Case Task Force reviewed them one by one, he began to understand just what a peculiar case it was.

"Most serial killers have a type," Gemma said. "There's always a pattern. The victims in this case are both men and women, and from various backgrounds, ages and ethnicities. The youngest was nineteen and the eldest was sixty-two. They include a freelance tax accountant, a landscaper, a lawyer, a contractor, and two people worked for different catering companies—one as a dishwasher and the other as a waitress."

"Lucy did occasional waitressing for cash under the table," Patrick said. Still, there weren't any obvious connections between the victims.

"So that might be three in catering," Caleb said. "It's not much but it's something."

"They're all contract jobs," Patrick said, the thought just occurring to him, "or at least, they could be."

That was one area where he guessed he had a lot more expertise and experience than anyone else on the call. More heads nodded.

"That's a smart observation," Gemma said, and Patrick felt warmth rise to the back of his neck.

"Only two died before they were dumped," Blake put in. "Both of those were shot. The rest died of exposure along with some combination of being choked, assaulted and suffering blunt force trauma. Some would've died of their injuries either way. Others were just wrapped up and left to die."

A shudder ran down Patrick's spine and his chest tightened. He couldn't imagine how terrifying that would be.

"So, it's possible there were more victims who were wrapped up in plastic and left for dead in the forest," Oscar said, "but who managed to escape and never reported it to law enforcement, which to me sounds like the work of an organized crime outfit."

"How did anyone conclude that this was the work of a serial killer?" Caleb asked. He blew out a hard breath and shook his head.

"Because of the plastic, the fact that all had similar bell tattoos, the location and the shoddy police work," Gemma said.

"Well, I'm good if we want to say Noëlville Serial *Killers* from now on instead of killer," Finnick added, "especially as we now have three unidentified men we suspect are involved. For all we know, the police and media jumped on the idea that there was this Noëlville Serial Killer out there, and Rust, Bone and Umber—whoever they are—just went with it."

And now they might have Tristan too. They needed to find his son.

"It's definitely possible," Jackson said. "Why bother coming up with a strategy to hide your crimes when the police and media do it for you with a flashy serial killer moniker you can hide behind?"

A deep and disgusted sigh left his chest that seemed to echo around the call.

"Also, we've got a bizarre new wrinkle to the tattoo clue," Gemma said, She glanced to Patrick. "Tell them what you told me."

"Lucy got a tattoo of a Christmas bell on her ankle when

Tristan was born," Patrick said. "Eleven months before she disappeared."

"Fourteen months before her body was found," Gemma added. "So, I think it's pretty safe to assume that the Noëlville killers didn't put it there, and that the initial investigation was wrong to think it started out as a serial killer's calling card."

The sharp inhale of breath that spread around the room was palpable, as if somebody had simultaneously sucker-punched them in the gut at once.

"Wait!" Lucas called. "I think I found something relevant!"

He set his phone down, there was the sound of papers flying and books shuffling, and then he came back. There was a spiral notebook in his hand. He flipped a page.

"I've been going over all of the autopsy reports and pictures," Lucas said, "and I noticed that none of the reports for the second victim mentioned the bell tattoo. So, I went over every picture of the body with painstaking detail, and sure enough I couldn't find a tattoo. But the victim was found just ten months after Lucy in the same stretch of French River Provincial Park, outside Noëlville, and the media was quick to call it a potential serial killer. Then eight months later, victim three shows up with the tattoo and every victim onward."

"That's brilliant work," Finnick said.

"So, the original case files say that every victim had the same tattoo," Caleb said. There was so much disgust in his voice as he said the word *original*—it might as well have meant *garbage*. "But in reality, it was only the first one, third one and then the rest. For all we know, our killers caught wind of the serial killer rumors and decided to use the tattoo to make people think it was the work of a single serial killer. Create a boogeyman for people to fear and distract from their crime."

Gemma got up from her seat and moved beside Patrick. "I

want to research something." She turned her camera off and her fingers flew over her phone again, so quickly he couldn't even catch what she was writing. She leaned toward him so that everybody on the screen could see her face.

"Gabe said that Missy was going to take Tristan to 'hit' a place in Noëlville," she told the group. Her fingers made air quotes. "Says it's the last big target before she gives up the 'life,' so I'm guessing she's planning on robbing a pretty big target. Maybe I can figure out where."

Missy was going to use his son to help commit a robbery? He shuddered at the thought.

"But how can we possibly figure out where she's planning to make a robbery?" Patrick asked. He turned toward Gemma and his shoulder bumped against hers.

"Missy and Gabe have criminal records for theft," she said. Her eyes were locked on the phone. Words and windows appeared and disappeared on the screen in a blur. "You told me Lucy had a problem with stealing too and had plans to work a party with them when she disappeared. Now we can assume that somebody recently stole something valuable that Rust, Bone and Umber are after, and that it was stolen by somebody who'd rather pay goons to do their dirty work for them than call the cops." Her fingers clicked. "And I've got it."

Moments later he heard a swoosh, followed by the sound of everybody's phone pinging at once. He opened he link she'd sent. It was the website to a very fancy event hall called the Holly Jolly Ranch. Set on top of a high hill, in between Noëlville and North Bay, it appeared to specialize in year-round Christmas-themed events.

Something prickled at the back of Patrick's neck. He recognized that building! But where did he know it from?

Lord, help me remember.

"'Privacy and Discretion Guaranteed,'" Oscar read the

block-letter words on the bottom of the screen out loud and snorted. "I assume they mean celebrities won't be harassed by paparazzi. But it could also mean 'we'll turn a blind eye to criminal activity as long as you pay enough.' I wonder why it's never been raided by the vice squad."

"At least now I know where I can spend thousands of dollars throwing an elaborate Christmas-in-July garden party," Caleb said, dryly, "complete with snow machines and sleighs pulled by fake horses. What was your search criteria, Gemma?"

"I was looking for somebody wealthy, in between the triangle of Noëlville, Sudbury and North Bay, who was recently robbed and didn't want the police involved," Gemma said. "I was honestly looking for a person. Maybe a wealthy family. But this was the only place that hit the mark."

A memory clicked in the back of Patrick's mind. He leaped to his feet.

"I know that place!" he said. "They have a reputation for using a lot of temporary outside contractors because they're easier to fire than permanent staff. I've actually done a few one-off construction projects for this place. They're constantly putting out calls to local construction and landscaping firms to help with larger-scale events, so they rely on local handymen for quick builds. I haven't done very many. But I know the main guys who do. It's very good money for a one-off."

Patrick bounced on the balls of his feet, feeling fresh energy fill his body along with a renewed sense of hope. Were there any construction or landscaping projects going on right now? If so, did he know anyone working on them? The sun had only been up an hour—and this could lead them to his son.

"I want to check on something," Patrick told Gemma.

She nodded and moved to sit next to her brother. Patrick turned his camera off and began to search the message boards, while keeping one ear out for the team as they continued to talk.

"I can see records for a handful of times when police got called out for incidents at the Holly Jolly Ranch but were then turned away," Gemma told the team. "Each time it was because somebody called 911 but didn't give their name. One was two days before Lucy's death and another was three weeks ago. My theory is that whoever booked the Holly Jolly Ranch that night has something to do with the Noëlville Serial Killers. Maybe something went down at an event each of those nights—a robbery or a fight—and whoever had booked Holly Jolly's facilities that night decided they didn't want police involved and so each one was swept under the rug."

"I see three problems with this," Caleb said.

"Hit me," Gemma said. She leaned back and crossed her arms.

"The first is that you're accusing a Christmas-themed ranch of killing people," he admitted. "That's pretty out there."

"No," Gemma said. "I'm accusing somebody who booked or attended parties there of being in the habit of solving their problems in a way that doesn't involve police. That doesn't mean all the victims were killed in this area either. Maybe only a handful were, and the rest could've been transported here after death to keep up the Noëlville Serial Killer facade. As for why it's never been raised, it actually looks like Holly Jolly Ranch has a great relationship with law enforcement most of the time. According to an article online, the police commissioner held his daughter's wedding there. It's only been a handful of times when police were turned away for so-called 'false alarms,' because somebody 'accidentally' called 911," Gemma went on, dryly. "And that might not be on the venue. It's not like they're going to accuse their clients of lying to police."

Patrick scrolled through the online postings for one-off construction jobs. Nobody he knew was online. But Holly Jolly Ranch had posted a few ads for holiday workers.

"Okay," Caleb said. "Second problem. It would mean that Missy hit the same location more than once, even after her friend got killed."

"Criminals are dumb," Oscar said.

"A surprising number of them return to the scene of a crime," Blake chimed in.

"Wealthy targets," Jackson added, "easy access."

"And according to Simcoe," Gemma said, "Missy smells like drugs."

Patrick kept scrolling. Looked like Holly Jolly had been trying to find a lot of construction guys for a very big Christmas Eve winter wonderland event.

"Okay, you got me on that one." Caleb held his hands up in defeat. "But my third problem is that a venue like Holly Jolly Ranch is not going to hand over their client list without a warrant. They might have a good relationship with police, but they'll also have lawyers who aren't going to be down to cut corners, especially if they're secretive about their client list. That takes time, and we've got a missing kid to worry about. We can't just waltz through the front gate, poke around every corner and start asking questions."

"Maybe *you* can't." Patrick stepped behind Jackson and joined him and Gemma on camera. "But I can. A place like that uses a lot of contractors, and I've got a lot of connections in this area. If you can drive me up to the service entrance, I guarantee I can get in and get answers."

NINE

The front entrance of the Holly Jolly Ranch had huge, ornate stone gates, with iron bars and towering marble sculptures of reindeer and candy canes. Jackson slowed his truck as they passed, so they could take in the gaudy splendor of it all.

Gemma, Jackson and Patrick had packed up and hit the road within moments of their call ending earlier. Despite, his insistence that he'd be fine going in alone, the team quickly agreed that Jackson and Hudson would go in with him, while Gemma stayed outside the ranch with Simcoe and did surveillance via drone. Hudson was a top-notch search and rescue dog. If Tristan was anywhere on the property, the K-9 would find him.

They'd sorted out the rest of the details as they drove, with Caleb acting as Jackson's navigator, letting them know which roads were open. The snowplows hadn't reached many of the rural areas, and there was still a maze of fallen trees, branches and power lines to navigate. But now, a few hours later, here Gemma was sitting in the passenger seat and checking messages from the team, as Jackson searched for Holly Jolly's service entrance.

Not to mention she was also focusing really hard on not continually stealing glances behind her to where Patrick now sat with the dogs in the back seat. She wasn't exactly sure what it was about his face that kept drawing her eyes. Between the accidental face bump and the unusually long hug, there'd been two inexplicably awkward moments between them so far, and now she could add to that the fact her heart was thudding up a ruckus at the idea of him being the one who was going to go in undercover at Holly Jolly to see what he could find out.

Jackson drove higher up the hill. The truck slowed to a stop, and she looked up to see a nearly imperceivable unpaved road cutting into the woods, noticeable only by the fact someone had cleared it of snow. A drop arm barrier was visible down the road through the trees. Security cameras stood tall on imposing poles, and Gemma noticed that Jackson had intentionally stopped before the truck came into the lenses' view. Three metal signs hung on a tall fence topped with barbed wire. A large red one announced it was Private Property, a second yellow one announced Trespassers Will Be Prosecuted, and a smaller white one read Holly Jolly Ranch.

"Anything new from the team?" Jackson asked.

"No." Gemma frowned. Unfortunately, research took time, and that was before accounting for the fact that a lot of the people outside the team who they'd be contacting for information were out for the holidays. "A lot of work has been done. Just not a lot of results. Amy's completed her sketches of Umber, Rust and Bone, and they're really good. You should find a copy in your email to show people along with current pictures of Missy. Caleb compared them against the main criminal databases and hasn't gotten a hit. Lucas compared them against Holly Jolly's staff page. No hits there either. But he also confirmed that the venue uses an external and highly reputable private security firm who uses retired cops, and I doubt they're on the venue's payroll. So that's a dead end, for now. According to Blake, potential sightings have been pouring in for Missy and Tristan, but nothing solid or promising yet. Also, a lot of people in Ontario are still without phone or electricity. We might get more tips as more people get online."

In other words, Patrick's plan of just striding through the service entrance, and using his own reputation and contacts in the community to get information out of the contractors and grounds people, was still the best option. And something inside Gemma's gut hated it. Even though he'd have an undercover cop and K-9 by his side, she couldn't think of a better option, and she was the last person on the team to argue against civilians stepping in to help where they could. Considering that Tristan was Patrick's child, an entire army probably couldn't stop him, if there was even a sliver of a hope that somebody inside had any idea how he could find his son.

Jackson had also given Patrick both his bulletproof vest to wear under his jacket along with a radio in case they lost cell phone signal. On top of that, Gemma would be piloting Jackson's drone over the site once he was inside, to get visual confirmation. Not to mention, she'd be watching the whole thing with Jackson's drone.

And yet, something inside her heart was practically yelling at her that this whole thing was a bad idea. Something about this plan terrified her—but she didn't know what.

Jackson seemed to sense it to, because as Patrick got changed into the bulletproof vest in the backseat of the truck, her brother signaled for her to get out and follow him a few feet down the road.

"Don't worry." Jackson leaned toward her, once they'd walked far enough away that they wouldn't be overheard. "He's going into a situation where he obviously feels comfortable, talking to people he's familiar with, and I'll be right by his side."

"I know," she admitted.

But convincing her racing heart was a whole other matter.

I'm feeling scared and I don't know why. Is it just my nerves? Or is something actually wrong? And if so, why can't I see it?

"You really care about Patrick, don't you?" Jackson asked.

"I don't want to talk about my feelings for him," Gemma said, instinctively and broke her brother's gaze. "It's not relevant."

"Are you sure?" Jackson asked. "I know whenever Amy or Skye are in danger it can impact my ability to think straight."

That was different. Jackson and Amy were in love. They were married. He'd been there for his adopted daughter, Skye, since the day she was born. Besides, Gemma didn't want to confirm that she liked Patrick but didn't exactly know how to deny it. There was something about Patrick that just drew her in. He had the kind of rugged strength that a person got from working with all his might to deal with everything life threw at him, while also facing more challenges than anyone should ever have to deal with. And yet, it hadn't made him hard or cold. If anything, he was like a rock with a warm molten core.

"Gem," Jackson said, softly, "if I thought he was walking into active danger I'd stop him. I promise you that."

"I know," Gemma said. She glanced back at him. "I don't quite know how to say this, but sometimes the memory of what happened a year and a half ago, when that killer was chasing after me, fills my mind like it's all happening again. I feel terrified and I freeze."

Something softened in her brother's blue eyes. She braced herself for a lecture.

"I'm sorry," Jackson said.

Two words. That was all. And somehow those were all the words she needed her brother to say.

"I'm sorry too," she said. "I feel like I can never apologize enough for the fact I disappeared on you and Amy like that, and let you think I was dead."

"I know." Jackson said. "But I get why you did it and we've both changed a lot since then."

The sound of the door opening and closing turned their attention back to the truck. Patrick had stepped out. Jackson patted her on the shoulder and then walked over to join Patrick.

"All good?" Jackson called.

"All good!" Patrick's chin rose and determination shone in his eyes.

"Remember," Jackson added, "your goal is to find somebody you know you can trust and ask them what they know. We don't know who's all involved in this and if any of the staff are compromised."

Patrick nodded. Jackson got Tristan's boots out of the truck and ordered Hudson to search for the scent. But even though the K-9 sniffed diligently, the German shepherd didn't detect anything. But maybe they'd find something inside the ranch.

Gemma got back in the truck, Simcoe climbed into the front seat beside her, and together they watched as Patrick, Jackson and Hudson sauntered up to the back gate. Patrick was pushing the call box button for security.

"Hello?" The answering voice was flat, male and distorted by the speaker.

"Hey, can you let Gino on the construction crew know that Patrick is here to help with his forklift situation?" Patrick braced one hand on the box and leaned forward. "He really needs to replace that thing. It seizes up in cold weather. He might as well just use a pulley system."

There was a pause. Then another buzz and the metal gate swung open.

The trio disappeared down the road into the trees and were gone.

"Now, that was a neat trick," Jackson's voice crackled over the radio. "Guess it pays to know what you're talking about."

The sound of footsteps crunched on the gravel for a moment, then an indistinct chorus of men shouting greetings filled the radio.

"Merry Christmas, Gino!" Patrick shouted.

"Hello, Patrick!" Laughter filled Gino's voice. "What are you doing on the mainland?"

"I was in the area visiting friends," Patrick said. "This is my buddy Jackson and his dog Hudson. Saw your crew was working the Holly Jolly gig and thought I'd swing by in case you needed a spare hand. How are you going to get those lights up on the platform with a forklift like that?"

"Eh, we got muscle power!"

It was the kind of light easy banter that floated between people who knew each other through work.

Gemma let out a long breath. Okay, so they'd made it in.

The voices blended into a chorus, overlapping with each other, as people greeted Patrick, Jackson and Hudson, wished them a Merry Christmas and asked Patrick's advice on the various things they were working on. So far, so good. Gemma drove farther down the road, parked in the trees and then got out the drone. It looked a bit like a four-legged daddy longlegs spider, with long spokes that jutted out from a small central camera, each of which had a propeller on the end. The controller was a cross between a tablet computer and Tristan's LMNTL game, with two knobs to direct the flight path and a screen to watch the camera feed. Gemma got out of the truck and carefully set the drone on the roof. She fiddled the dials, and it lifted off and took flight high over the trees.

Casual conversation pattered down the radio, growing

more serious as Patrick said casually. "My ex has a friend who's a bit...off." He blew out a hard breath. "Tristan was hanging out with her and she didn't bring him back when she was supposed to. I don't want to get her in trouble, I just want Tristan home."

Smart way of putting it. Got across all the important information while not raising unnecessary alarm in case somebody there knew Missy. One could never be sure who knew who in small-town rural communities.

Her eyes stayed locked on the screen casting the drone's camera feed. For a moment all she saw were the tops of snow-covered trees, with fleeting glimpses of white powdery ground. Then the trees parted, and she was flying over the sweeping grounds of Holly Jolly Ranch, with its towering stone pillars, huge patios, walled gardens and what looked like dozens and dozens of wooden holiday-shaped structures wrapped in miles of unlit Christmas lights. The main parking lot was empty, and the place looked deserted except for a flurry of grounds crew setting up for the event that night. People in white jackets carried silver-covered platters out of catering trucks.

Moments later, she spotted Patrick, Jackson and Hudson standing with a small group of mostly men, who were working to erect what looked like a complicated holiday grotto.

Patrick was passing his phone among the workers, likely showing pictures of Tristan, or photos of Missy they'd pulled off social media earlier. Conversation continued to patter in her ear.

Then a large man, some six-foot-five in a plaid jacket, with a huge white beard and shoulder-length hair, placed a hand on Patrick's shoulder.

"Hey Pat," the man said. "Let me show you something inside."

"Hey, Chuck," Patrick greeted the man. "Sure."

Quickly, she searched for him online. Fortunately, he and Patrick were fast friends on social media. Chuck Brown had been working construction jobs in and around North Bay for almost fifty years. He was looking for a buyer for an offshoot business he owned in Barrie. Good reputation. No criminal record.

No red flags.

Then how to explain the palpable sense of terror Gemma could still feel climbing up her spine? Something was wrong. Every fiber of her being was practically telling her so. Even though there was no proof that was true.

Gemma watched on the screen as Chuck and Patrick started toward the main building. Jackson followed one step behind, with Hudson by his side, when suddenly the bearded man turned back and held up a hand.

"Nothing personal," Chuck told Jackson, "but this is a two man conversation."

Something in the older man's tone, even via radio, told her it wasn't up for debate. Whatever he wanted to show Patrick, he didn't want an audience, A warning shiver ran down Gemma's spine. Why would Chuck want to talk to Patrick alone?

No Jackson, you can't let him do this.

"It's cool," Patrick told Jackson. "I've known this guy for over a decade. Good man. Good heart. Strong family. He's like a dad to me."

"You sure you don't need us?" Jackson kept his voice light and casual, but Gemma could hear the hint of concern in its depths.

"Yeah." Patrick's voice was so firm it could've cut glass. "Trust me. It's all good."

Jackson hesitated for a moment. Then, to her dismay, her brother stepped aside and watched as Patrick followed the man over the snow and toward the imposing main building. It was shaped like an oversized and whimsical ski chalet. Smoke billowed from a huge central brick chimney. But as far as her instincts were concerned it might as well be a deep and dark dungeon. She watched as Chuck and Patrick walked up two sets of imposing front steps and through a huge double wooden door. The drone hovered over the building as the two men disappeared inside.

Casually, Jackson took a few steps toward the tree line, away from anyone working the grounds who might overhear their conversation. Then he pulled his phone to his ear.

"How could you?" Gemma asked him, knowing he could hear her in his earpiece and was using the phone just for cover so people didn't see him talking to himself.

"How could I let Patrick talk privately with a man he trusted and had known for years, instead of risking blowing his cover and tanking the whole investigation?" Jackson asked. It was rhetorical. "Did you check Chuck online?"

"Obviously," Gemma said. "No red flags."

But the man was still leading Patrick away from the others and into a place where it was a lot harder to get a visual. There was the sound of footsteps echoing on the marble floor of what sounded like a cavernous room.

"Okay, you can't tell anyone I showed you this," she heard Chuck say, "or we'll both be in a lot of trouble."

Then the radio cut out and static filled the line.

Gemma felt lightheaded. "We've completely lost the signal."

Suddenly, the ring of a telephone filled the cab, jolting her attention. It was Finnick.

"He's calling me too," Jackson said.

She muted the radio and answered the call, as Jackson joined it too.

"Hey," her boss said. "We've got a solid lead on the kid, but we have to act quickly and handle it with care."

Gemma silently thanked God, as her heart leaped in her chest.

"I got a call from Gabriel's probation officer," Finnick went on. "Apparently, Gabriel is with Missy and Tristan now at a trailer about ten minutes' drive from your location. Gabriel doesn't know how long he'll be able to stall them for, and he's worried that Missy will panic and do something drastic at the sight of cops. The last thing we want is this to turn into a hostage situation or for her to grab Tristan and flee. I've put in a call to the provincial police, but the closest station in the area is over thirty-minutes away. We don't have a second to waste."

"Great news, small hitch," Jackson said. "Patrick's talking to a contact privately and we don't have visual."

"Well, go get him and get out there," Finnick said.

"On it," Jackson said.

She watched as Jackson and Hudson hurried toward the chalet and then went inside. For a long and tense moment she listened as Jackson, still on the line and connected to radio, looked for Patrick—casually at first and then growing more urgent as he called Patrick's name and footsteps rushed from room to room. Then, finally she heard Jackson command Hudson to search for him. The dog sniffed, then whimpered.

"I don't know how to explain it," Jackson said, "but I've lost him. According, to Hudson his scent just vanishes in a random hallway partway through the building. Patrick's gone."

TEN

They'd lost both audio and visual connection with Patrick, and now Hudson couldn't even find his scent. Where was he? What had happened to him?

"This might be our only chance to save the boy," Finnick said. Pain and frustration filled his voice. "Tristan has to be our priority. I hate to do this, but I need you to get out of there and go find and rescue him."

"Understood," Jackson said. He'd be on his way back now.

"I'm staying," Gemma said. "We can't just leave Patrick here alone."

Finnick paused for a moment and she suspected he was both praying and ruing the fact the snow and roads had left her and Jackson without more backup.

"Agreed," Finnick said. "We're not about to leave a man behind. Gemma, stay there with the drone, find shelter and wait for Patrick to get in contact. Take Simcoe with you. Caleb is forty-minutes out and I'll send him to find you. Jackson, you go pick up Tristan and make sure he's safe. Nippy and I are on our way from the island. I should be with you within the hour too."

"Got it," Jackson and Gemma said in unison.

She leaped out of the truck with Simcoe by her side, being careful to keep the drone hovering steady, and just in time to see Jackson and Hudson burst through the trees. Her brother's eyes met hers. Moments later Jackson and Hudson climbed into the truck and took off, leaving her alone in the snow with Simcoe.

Lord, please keep Patrick safe. Help us protect him.

Finnick ended the call with the promise to be in touch soon and the reminder to pray. Backup would be there soon. She turned back to the controls.

"I'm going to use the drone to try to find Patrick," she told Simcoe. "But if I can't, we're going in."

No matter what Finnick had said. Simcoe woofed softly. She focused on the screen. Now all she had to do was get eyes inside the building. She strongly doubted anyone was about to let her just fly a surveillance drone through the front door.

But fortunately there was more than one way in the building.

All she needed was the skill to pull it off.

She moved the drone over the chimney and positioned it directly over the square gap in the brick. Smoke blinded her visual from the feed. She heard the propellers knock and scrape against the brick walls she couldn't see. Then the orange glow of the flames appeared below her, growing closer and closer until the entire screen was enveloped in a wall of dancing flames.

She sucked in a breath. Red-and-green-striped holiday stockings hovered to her right. She steered the drone toward them and pushed the speed as fast as it would go. The drone shot out of the fireplace, snagging itself on a string of holly that hung over the fireplace mantel and dragging it along in its wake as it flew through a huge ballroom.

Not exactly stealth mode.

She and the rest of the team would probably laugh later about the vision of a drone flying around the Holly Jolly

Ranch, dragging an unknown quantity of greenery and bows behind it like a bizarre Christmas comet. But not now. Not until she found Patrick. Not until she knew for certain he was safe.

The room was empty. No people, but dozens and dozens of evergreen trees lined the walls, decked out in shiny silver baubles.

She gritted her teeth and focused on the screen.

Come on, Patrick. Where are you?

The hall was lined with tall fiberglass candy canes. An archway lay ahead. She gritted her teeth and flew through into a circular foyer dominated by a gigantic grandfather clock. A wooden staircase lay to her right. She turned to face it. Someone was running down the stairs. She saw boots, a brown wool coat, a face with short-cropped hair and then a fedora.

It was Rust.

Rust raised a gun, set the drone in his sights and fired.

She heard a bang, then watched as the drone spiraled down in a nosedive and crashed into the floor. Then the screen went black.

A muffled bang came from somewhere beyond the thick oak-lined walls that surrounded Patrick on all sides. But it was so faint, he couldn't begin to guess what it was.

"Wow, the soundproofing in here is mind-blowing," Patrick said to Chuck. "The world outside could probably explode and I wouldn't be able to hear it. This place is…unbelievable."

Not to mention slightly terrifying. In all his years of construction, Patrick had never seen anything quite like the Stroke of Midnight Room. They'd entered it via a secret entrance that had led to a tunnel that was hidden behind a large grandfather clock in the foyer.

He trusted Chuck with his life and on a good day would've

found it pretty funny. But now, all he could think was whether his son was trapped somewhere like this. The tunnel had slanted downward, but he had no idea how deep underground they'd gone. The room itself was windowless, with dark wood panels that stopped just a foot short of the dark blue ceiling. There were no visible doors either, just a few small and well-hidden hinges tucked between two panels. It was empty except for three round tables surrounded by four chairs each, an empty bar and a plain gold artificial tree in one corner. The whole effect was imposing and intimidating.

"Yeah," Chuck said and shook his head, like even he was surprised by the place where he'd led Patrick. "I wouldn't be surprised if 99 percent of the people who pass through this building have no idea that this room is even here. The construction crews and service people aren't supposed to know about it, but the walls are lined with metal, and it caused a problem with the wiring that triggers the door and connects to the security system. I had to sign a nondisclosure agreement. They could sue me within an inch of my life for even telling you about this place."

Chuck laughed. But Patrick smiled weakly. He'd never been in a room he'd been so eager to get out of. It smelled of stale cigarettes, alcohol and heavy perfume. And while he didn't want to even imagine the kind of events that someone would book a room like this for, he couldn't shake the feeling that something very bad had happened here. Probably more than once.

He glanced down at his phone, feeling the urge to fire a quick and subtle text off to Gemma and let her know what was going on. Only then did he realize that he didn't have a signal anymore either. Right, the walls were lined with metal. The room itself was a Faraday cage. And he'd just stepped right into it.

"So why are we here?" Patrick asked.

"This place needed to be seen to be believed," the construction worker said. Chuck sighed sadly and Patrick watched as what looked like a silent prayer crossed his lips. "You're a good man, Patrick, and it's hard for guys to imagine why a place like this would even exist. You needed to see it to get it, and so I wanted to show you this room myself instead of just trying to explain it to you." He blew out a hard breath and his smile faded. "A venue like this keeps a No Entry/Do Not Hire list, of people who are permanently banned from the premises. Certain groundskeepers, catering staff, housekeeping and maintenance can get blacklisted from a place like this for being incompetent, drunk or inappropriate."

"Or getting caught stealing," Patrick added.

"Yeah," Chuck agreed. "I did hear there was a call out here last month because of a theft that happened in the Stroke of Midnight Room, which is what led to them wanting me to beef up the room's security. I'd seen Holly Jolly's No Entry/Do Not Hire list dozens of times. But when I was hired to work on this room, I was supplied with a secret no-entry list of which people had been specifically banned from working events in this room due to being suspected of stealing from guests during previous parties. As you can imagine, it's a much shorter list. Only half a dozen names, which makes it a lot easier to remember. Missy Kerry was on that list. She was added about a month ago."

"Wow." Patrick blew out a long breath. Was this the room that "the stash" had been stolen from? It certainly added up with what Gemma said about police being called to the venue recently only to be sent away. Maybe whoever was hosting the parties or had been robbed didn't want the police involved. So they'd sent Rust, Bone and Umber after the thief instead. "That's unbelievable."

Then, to his surprise, the frown lines on Chuck's face deepened.

"Missy wasn't the only one on the list," the older man said. "So was your gal, Lucy."

The words hit Patrick like a sucker punch to the chest. The party that Lucy and Missy had gone to work at was in this dark and dangerous-feeling room? Had they stolen from the excluded guests in this room, and it had gotten one of them killed?

"Hang on," Patrick said. "Missy apparently said she needed my son to rob someplace."

"Some big toy company is holding a giveaway tonight for over a thousand kids," Chuck said. "Expensive gear. Fancy newfangled electronic stuff. I saw the trucks pulling up earlier. I'm guessing that since Missy's name is on a banned list, she needs a child with her to get past security. Unless, she's planning on sending your kid in alone to steal stuff for her."

Either way, it meant Missy would be using Tristan to rob the Holly Jolly Ranch during the kids Christmas party. Patrick sighed.

"Well, now the cops will be on the lookout for any matching Missy or Tristan's description at the party tonight," Patrick said.

He could only hope and pray the police were able to get them and rescue Tristan before it was too late.

Chuck ran his hand over the back of his head. "I'm so sorry I wish I had better news."

"Hey, I'm just really thankful for everything you've shown me and told me," Patrick said, "I really appreciate it."

Only then did the older man smile again. "No problem. The missus and I will be praying that the police find your boy soon."

Chuck slid the door open, and they headed back up the tunnel, out from behind the grandfather clock and into the main foyer. The sun was setting deeper now behind tall domed windows. Chuck headed back outside through a back door to help the crew wrap up for the night's event. But Patrick paused in the foyer.

Father God, thank You for leading me this far. Please continue to guide me and show me Your Wisdom.

Then he pulled out his phone to call Gemma and started to walk back toward the front entrance. Only then did he see the mass of green garland, red ribbons and broken electronics lying on the floor beside the stairs and walked over to it.

It was the drone, and by the looks of things, somebody had shot it to smithereens.

Just like that his heart began to race again. He dialed Gemma's number.

"Patrick!" Her voice was breathless, and it sounded like she was running. "Are you okay? Where were you? What happened?"

"I'm fine," Patrick said. "I was in a hidden underground room that's even more dodgy than it sounds. I'll explain later. Are you okay?"

"We have a potential lock on Tristan," she said, and Patrick felt his breath catch painfully in his throat. "It's solid, but tricky. Gabriel was with Tristan and Missy in a nearby trailer, and Finnick said he was worried about a potential hostage situation. Jackson's heading there now to hopefully negotiate with Missy to let him go and bring him home."

Hope and fear battled in his chest. He made his way toward the front door, down the hallway, past tall fiberglass candy canes and into the large event space, where an indoor Christmas forest surrounded a towering fireplace.

"I'm still in the lodge and heading for the entrance," he said. "Where are you now?"

"A few yards away from the building," she said. "Jackson left me here with Simcoe to meet up with you. We found a hole in the fence and are on our way to you. But Rust is here too. I saw him coming down the stairs and he shot our—"

Her voice faded from his ears and the world froze, as Patrick heard the creak of footsteps in front of him combined with the simple metallic click of a bullet sliding into a chamber. Then Rust stepped through a doorway, barely three feet away from his noise. Patrick leaped, phone still in his hand, and threw himself at the man in the fedora just as Rust set Patrick in his sights and fired.

Patrick felt the bullet whizz past his ear as his shoulder caught the gunman in the middle, and he threw him hard against the ground. Rust fired again. A bullet ricocheted off the mantel, sending chunks of red brick flying. Silver baubles fell from the trees and smashed onto the ground.

Patrick dropped his phone inside his jacket pocket, clasped both hands around Rust's wrist and tried to wrestle the weapon from his grasp. Then he heard the sound of Gemma screaming his name echoing down the phone line.

ELEVEN

Desperately, Gemma shouted Patrick's name into the phone again, but all she heard were the muffled sounds of shouting and gunshots.

Lord, please keep Patrick safe! Help me reach him in time!

The lodge loomed ahead of her. Not that she had any idea what she was going to do when she got inside. She only knew that he was in trouble and she was going to make sure that he wasn't in danger alone.

The phone line had gone dead now. Quickly, she dialed Caleb, who answered on the first ring.

"Hey, Gemma." Caleb sounded worried. "No eyes on Tristan yet. The situation's getting tricky—"

"Patrick's under fire." Her words came out quick and short as she ran.

"Okay." He switched gears instantly. "I'm twenty-five minutes out. Just take cover and stay safe."

She'd called Caleb earlier to let him know Rust had shot the drone down. What he didn't know was that she'd since made her way through the fence.

"I'm on the grounds now," she said, "and making my way toward the main building. I'll keep you posted."

"Okay," Caleb said again, and it was only when he didn't argue that she realized just how worried he was.

"Is everything okay with Tristan?" she asked.

"No," he said bluntly. "But we haven't lost hope yet. Just focus on staying safe."

She ran faster through the snow, pressing through the trees toward the main building. Simcoe galloped by her side. Gemma glanced down at the dog, and, as if sensing her gaze, the kelpie looked up at her and woofed.

The sun was setting deeper below the horizon, and she saw long purple shadows spreading out across the freshly fallen snow. She burst through the trees and found herself on a long and winding driveway that led to the main building. Construction, catering and maintenance vehicles streamed down the drive, apparently skipping the service road and heading straight for the fastest exit. A maroon van with Gino's Construction on the side slowed down. A young man in a blue hat waved at her from the passenger window.

"Gunshots in the main building," the young man yelled. "They're clearing the place out and shutting everything down. Police are on their way."

"Thank you!" she shouted back.

The van pulled away toward the exit. She thanked God that police were coming, but any feeling of relief would wait until she knew Patrick was safe. She steeled a breath and kept running. Her legs burned. A security guard somewhere off to her left shouted something about an active shooter, but nobody moved to stop her as she sprinted up the stairs. A gunshot sounded to her right, exploding the window and sending a spray of glass cascading out into the snow.

She reached the huge front entrance, slipped through the front door and silently signaled Simcoe to stand beside her. The dog pressed against her leg, and Gemma reached down and ran a hand over the back of the K-9's neck. Then she paused and prayed for guidance. The heavy wooden door lay to her back. A long hallway bedecked with garlands and fiberglass candy canes lay ahead of her. For a moment, silence fell ahead of her, and the sounds of people peeling out of the lot outside faded too.

Lord, please give me wisdom.

A crash sounded ahead through a doorway. Then she heard Patrick call out in prayer to God for help.

She steeled a breath and started down the hall. The sound of a struggle rose ahead of her. She reached a doorway, braced herself for a moment behind the frame and then looked through.

Suddenly it was like time slowed to a crawl, stretching fractions of a second into minutes.

It was the room with the giant fireplace where she'd flown the drone. At first she could barely see past the maze of fallen trees. Broken baubles littered the ground. Wind whipped through the broken window.

She creeped forward silently and then she saw them. Patrick was down on the floor, on his back, fighting with the man in the fedora, who was crouching over him. The barrel of Rust's gun was aimed directly at the center of his forehead. One tiny wrong move of Rust's fingers was all it would take and Patrick would be killed in an instant.

For a second she stood there, paralyzed with fear.

Help me, Lord. Any movement I take could end Patrick's life!

Rust had his back to her and hadn't noticed she was there. But Patrick saw her. He looked up at Gemma, past the gun in his face and the killer threatening his life, and locked his gaze on her. And Gemma watched as trust filled Patrick's dark eyes.

Something warm and deep like liquid fire washed through her. The strongest and bravest person she'd ever met, Patrick

Craft, trusted her to save him. And knowing that gave her courage in a way she'd never felt before.

Her hands grasped one of the fiberglass candy canes that lined the hallway. She swung it around in front of her like a sword—

"Simcoe! Attack!"

Rust glanced back toward her, just as the fiberglass candy cane smashed him hard against the side of the head. Patrick wrenched his body sideways, and Simcoe locked her strong jaw on Rust's right hand, which held the gun. The weapon fired. The candy cane shattered. The bullet hit the floor mere inches away from Patrick's face and the wood exploded into splinters. A shadow moved past the broken window. A tall man with a fedora was running up the stairs toward the front door.

It was Umber.

Patrick grabbed Gemma's hand and pulled. "We've got to go!"

She glanced at Simcoe. The K-9 still hadn't released her grip on Rust, who was wailing in pain, and it was only the knowledge that Rust's backup would be here any second that caused Gemma to call the dog off. There wasn't time for the fight to disarm him. There was only time to run.

"Simcoe!" she shouted. "Come!"

The dog released her grip and ran to Gemma's side, just as Gemma and Patrick dashed into the hall. Gemma glanced to her right, just in time to see Umber arrive at the top of the stairs. A thick white bandage covered his nose, no doubt as a result of the walloping Patrick had given him in the woods the night before when he'd kidnapped her. Now two gunmen lay between them and the front door. Gemma, Patrick and Simcoe turned and ran back down the hallway, even as Umber fired after them, bullets ricocheting off the walls.

Her hand stayed tight in Patrick's grasp, as they burst side by side into the foyer, with a tall grandfather clock to one side and the staircase to another. The remains of her drone lay on the floor. Patrick led them around the staircase into a service hallway that led to a beautiful and long, shiny chrome kitchen. The heavy door swung shut behind them. She gasped a breath. Footsteps pounded down the hallway beyond. Did the men realize what room they'd ducked into? Would the men chase straight after them, or split up and try to cut them off?

An emergency exit lay ahead, in between long tables covered in Christmas goodies. She pulled her hand from Patrick's. They ducked low and ran for the exit single file, through a maze of magnificent gingerbread houses decked in icing and candies in every color of the rainbow. Bullets fired behind them. Gingerbread exploded in a haze of candy pieces and crumbs. But it was too late—they were already bursting outside into the snow again, feeling fresh winter air on their faces. They'd come out behind the building. Huge, manicured gardens spread out in front of them. It was only mid-afternoon, but already the sun had begun to set, turning the white snow to a deep shade of gray. It would be as dark as night by five.

"Caleb's on his way," she shouted. "All we have to do is find a place to hide until he can get here and rescue us."

But how to survive and stay alive until then? She glanced from left to right, looking for some way to escape or somewhere to hide.

Tall wooden structures rose out of the snow around them, wrapped in yards of unlit lights. They ran for them, weaving between the skeletal forms of snowmen, stockings and nutcrackers.

They stopped behind a large square object in the shape of a present with a bow on top and stooped low. Gemma's fingers brushed Simcoe's collar. Umber had burst through the back door and was searching for them. She didn't see Rust anywhere.

Or, for that matter, Bone.

"You said they found Tristan?" Patrick's words came out in whispered staccato in between shallow breaths.

She turned toward him but could barely see the lines of his face in the darkness.

"Yes," she said. "He's not far. Jackson's going to try and get him out."

Patrick inhaled deeply. "God, please help us. We need You."

It was a simple prayer but one that encompassed so much desperate need inside both their hearts.

"Amen," she whispered.

Suddenly, bright red and yellow bulbs switched on in front of them, drenching them in light. For a split second, she saw Patrick's handsome face illuminated in the glow, before turning to watch as structure after structure came alight, flooding the snow around them in dazzling color. So much for hiding in the shadows.

"They must be on a timer," Patrick whispered. "Come on. We've got to get out of here before he spots us."

She nodded, silently signaled to Simcoe and then followed Patrick across the brightly lit ground, darting between pools of blue, green, red and yellow lights.

"We've got to get out of here now!" Gemma shouted.

"This way!" Patrick called.

He darted through a shining white archway, and she saw the horse-drawn sleigh, like something out of a fantastical holiday movie. It was ornate, red and curved, covered in both jingle bells and lights, with two rows of velvet cushioned seats and huge golden runners.

Two realistic-looking white fiberglass horses were attached to the front, with their legs posed in a perpetual run and their hoofs a foot off the ground.

"What is that?" she asked.

Two angry voices shouted behind them now. Gunshots split the air. Decorations shattered around them, spilling broken bulbs across the snow.

"Our way out of here."

She watched as Patrick leaped over the edge of the sleigh and then reached back for her hand. She grabbed his hand, climbed up and called for Simcoe to jump up behind her. The dog leaped into the back seat and sat. Patrick sat down behind a pair of huge handlebars wrapped in red tinsel. She sat beside him and he gunned the engine. A single headlight beamed ahead of them between the horses. Twinkling Christmas lights flashed on all around them. It was only then that she realized they were sitting in an industrial-sized snowmobile that someone had converted into a sleigh.

The Christmas contraption shot forward across the snow, in a loud jangle of clanging bells. Shouts sounded behind them. She glanced back. Rust and Umber were running after them. Their weapons raised to shoot.

"Get down!" she shouted and grabbed Simcoe to duck low.

Bullets glanced off the back of the sleigh. The snowmobile-sleigh's single bright yellow headlight cut through the darkness ahead of them, but all she saw was trees.

"Hang on!" Patrick called. "We're going in."

"I don't see a path forward."

"We'll make one."

They flew toward forest. Wind whipped past them. A wall of gray and green branches filled her eyes. Then suddenly they burst into the trees. Pine needles scraped against the sides of the machine. Twigs snagged against the bells, creating a loud, discordant sound. The horses cracked and splintered as they smacked against the trees. For a brief moment of relief the sound of shouting faded from her ears, only to be replaced by what sounded like the roar of a smaller and sleeker snowmobile.

"We're making too much noise," Gemma said. "We're too easy to track!"

Not to mention they were decked with so many lights they might as well be driving a Christmas tree. She sat up, fished a pocket knife from inside her jacket, slid over to the side of the sleigh and began cutting the side decorations loose. A trail of jingle bells and lights spread out behind them in the snow. The snowmobile behind them roared louder. Then the glimmer of a headlight shone through the trees. The armed men were closing in.

She just had to get the lights on the other side, which would hopefully help them lose their pursuers.

"Try to keep it steady," she called. "I'm going to climb around into the back seat."

She glanced at Patrick. He quickly glanced her way—their eyes met for a split second—then he looked back and she watched as his jaw set.

"Stay safe," he said, "okay?"

"I will."

Carefully, she braced her hands on the back of the seat, slid over on her stomach and landed on her hands and knees beside Simcoe. The K-9's warm tongue licked her cold face in greeting. Gemma ran her hand over the dog's fur.

"Good dog," she said, softly. "Stay down."

She made her way to the other side of the sleigh and began to cut off the lights and bells. Branches flew low over her head. The runners bumped and jolted over rocks.

Then the final lights and bells were gone. Silence fell around them, except for the sound of the snowmobile rushing through the trees. But just as she was about to whisper a prayer of thanks, she heard a loud crack, the whole sleigh shuddered for a moment before it kept moving, and the beam of light that had pierced the darkness ahead of them suddenly went out.

"Everything okay?" she asked.

"Yeah." Determination and concern filled Patrick's deep voice in equal measure. "But one of the horses broke off and it took out the headlight. We're driving blind."

The ground sloped steeply beneath them. The snowmobile was picking up speed as the runners slid on the slippery ground. She felt herself pitching forward and had to brace herself against the seat in front of her. She tried to get her bearings, looking for the fence line that would take them back to the road and Caleb. Gemma glanced back. Darkness spread out behind them.

"I think we've lost them—" she started to say.

But suddenly, the ground slipped out from under them, like an invisible hand had grabbed the snowmobile-sleigh and tossed it into the sky. They'd hit a ledge somewhere in the snow—invisible in the darkness—and now they were plunging over it.

Instinctively, Gemma threw her arms around Simcoe and hugged the dog tight. Then she felt Patrick reach over the back of the seat and wrap his strong arms around them both.

The snowmobile spun in the darkness, and they fell through the air with no idea how long it would be until they hit the ground. Her stomach dropped. Prayers for safety filled her heart and poured over her lips. Patrick tucked her and Simcoe tighter into his chest.

Help us, Lord!

***

They were flying, spinning, helpless through the air. Patrick gritted his teeth, held on to Gemma with all his might and prayed.

Then with a jolt the sleigh hit the ground again and they pitched forward. Gemma was wrenched from his arms as their bodies flew out of the snowmobile.

He landed in the snowbank and sunk in deep. The air was knocked out of him. Patrick gasped and felt freezing air hit his lungs. He struggled to his feet.

"Gemma!" He forced a deep and painful breath. "Simcoe! Are you okay?"

"Patrick! I'm here."

He stumbled through the snow toward the sound of her voice, then heard Simcoe's loud and triumphant woof resounding through the chilly night air. Relief filled his heart.

"Everybody alright and in one piece?" he called.

"Seems so," Gemma called back.

A moment later and they'd reached each other. He felt Simcoe's furry head barrel into his legs then butt against his hand as he reached to pat her. Then he heard Gemma's footsteps come to a stop in front of him. A soft yellow light switched on, and he saw Gemma standing just a foot away. Something warm swelled in his heart. She was looking down at her phone. There was the whoosh and ping of texts being sent and received, then she slid her phone into her jacket's front so that the gentle glow of its light enveloped them both.

"I've just texted Caleb," she said. "He says he's got our location on GPS and is on his way to get us. He's hoping Jackson will join us with Tristan."

He whispered a prayer of thanksgiving under his breath.

The men in fedoras were nowhere in sight. Help was on its way. His son, Tristan, would be back, home and safe with him soon. The nightmare they'd been trapped in was almost over. Simcoe sighed contently and lay down in the snow by his feet. Patrick looked at Gemma. Her eyes were locked on his face.

"Are you okay?" he asked, softly.

"Yeah," she said. "That was an unexpected wipeout, but not the worst I've ever taken. Jackson and I used to sled some pretty gnarly hills. Now, what was this you were saying about a secret room in the lodge?"

He chuckled, feeling relief fill his chest. How long had she been waiting to ask him that?

"It was hidden behind a clock," he said, "and I suspect is used for pretty unsavory private parties with gambling and drugs. Both Lucy and Missy worked parties there and were involved in some kind of theft or something."

"Not bad sleuthing for a civilian." She punched him lightly in the arm.

He searched her face, as a feeling as if he'd just blindly opened a door to unexpectedly find an incredible treasure inside.

The kind of riches he'd never expected to find and now couldn't even believe were actually real.

"You ran toward gunfire for me." His voice barely rose above whisper. "What were you thinking?"

"That you were in danger," she admitted and blushed slightly. "And I was going to make sure that you didn't go through it alone."

He opened his mouth, expecting to find words there to say in response. When he didn't, he closed it again.

"You would've done the same for me," she added.

"Of course I would," he said. "I just can't imagine anyone doing something like that for me. Then again, I've never known how to ask anyone for help."

"I get it," she said, and smiled weakly. The beautiful flush in her cheeks deepened. "I let my own brother and my best friend think I was dead rather than ask for help. Thankfully, they've forgiven me. But still, I can't believe I was so determined to solve everything on my own back then."

"See, I actually get that," he admitted. "I could imagine doing the same."

"I'm glad I'm not the only one."

For a moment they just stood together, with their feet inches apart, in the crisp winter air. Patrick found himself pulling off his gloves, reaching up and cupping her cheek in his hand. Her blue eyes widened. She leaned into his hand, and an unusual warmth spread through his fingers into his core.

"Seriously, thank you for being there for me," Gemma said. She stepped toward him. "And thank you for listening to me. I feel like you're the first person who's actually really understood me."

"I get it," Patrick said. When Lucy had disappeared on him, Patrick's mother had practically begged him to move in with her and his dad and let them help him care for Tristan. Not to mention all the interesting women she'd tried to introduce to him over the years, to join his and Tristan's lives. But Patrick had been determined to do it alone. He'd never even asked them to babysit for him. Maybe because he felt like he'd made this mess by choosing Lucy and didn't deserve anyone's help now. But he'd never asked Gemma for help. She'd just shown up in his life and insisted on being there for him. His fingers gently brushed her neck. "It's hard to trust anyone, or let anyone else in, when you're used to being alone."

"Even when you want to," Gemma said.

"Yeah," Patrick said. "Especially when you want to."

She reached for him, wrapping her arms around his waist and hugging him tightly. Patrick's hand slid around the back of her neck. His fingers fanned through her hair. Then he bent toward her, she tipped her chin up toward him and their lips met in a sweet and simple kiss.

A sharp and judgmental thought in the recesses of his mind told him he needed to stop and step back. He hadn't kissed anyone since Lucy. And Gemma deserved a better man than him. Kissing her was impulsive, foolish and reckless. It had to be an odd reaction to the relief of being safe and alive, nothing more. Maybe even a mixture of needing someone to help him with the pain of losing his son and the hope Tristan might not be safe.

And yet, she didn't pull away. Neither did he. Instead, he hugged her closer to him. Her arms crept higher up his back.

Too late, the sound of Simcoe's warning growls reached his ears. Something moved in the trees. Then a sharp and piercing pain filled his body, like a thousand jellyfish, stinging his body and paralyzing him at once. He'd been hit with a stun gun. One set illegally high. Suddenly, unconsciousness swept over him, as powerfully and overwhelmingly as a tsunami wave. Blackness filled his eyes. Gemma was snatched away from his arms. Her screams echoed around him from every direction at once. And the last conscious thought his mind was able to grasp was Gemma telling Simcoe to hide. Then, everything went black.

TWELVE

Patrick woke up lying on his back, freezing cold and unable to move. His feet were bound together at the ankles. His hands were stuck to his sides. His mouth was gagged and something was wrapped so tightly around his chest he could barely breathe.

Panic filled his throat.

Where was he? What had happened? Where was Gemma? Where was Tristan?

He closed his eyes tightly and fought the terror battling inside him. Hours ago, when the sun had risen that morning, Gemma had told him she'd been praying and focusing on a verse from the Bible, Philippians 4.

"The peace of God," he spoke the words out loud into the darkness, "which passeth all understanding, shall keep your hearts and minds through Christ Jesus."

Then he forced a deep breath into his lungs, opened his eyes again and tried to take stock of what was happening.

Judging by the cold filling his limbs, he was still outside. He searched the silence, listening intently, and heard something that sounded like the rush of wind moving through the trees. Slowly, his eyes adjusted to the darkness, but he saw only indistinct shapes, like there was something distorting his field of vision. He moved his jaw but couldn't dislodge the gag from his mouth. He rocked violently from side to side then heard a scrunching sound, and finally the reality of the situation he was in came into clear, brutal and terrifying focus.

Only a few of the Noëlville Serial Killer's victims were killed before they were dumped. Most died of exposure after being left in the woods, injured and wrapped up in plastic.

Bound in plastic and left to die.

Just like him. Hot and angry tears pressed at the back of Patrick's lids, as he fought in vain against the bonds that held him fast. The thick plastic over his face and binding his arms seemed to tighten as panic threatened to take hold. Was this how Lucy had died? Trapped and alone?

In the chaos of everything that had happened in the past day and a half, he'd never taken a moment to really stop and think about how Lucy had died.

He'd never once gone looking for her after she'd left him. He'd been too angry, too hurt and above all so busy blaming himself for the fact he'd chosen to have a child with a woman who'd never really loved him and had been so quick to leave him.

Lord, forgive me for not looking for her...

It wasn't that he thought he could've saved her life. He'd tried and failed over and over again, to stop her from taking the path that had led her to working with her friend Missy in the kind of parties they'd held in the Stroke of Midnight Room, and stealing from the kind of entity who'd send Rust, Bone and Umber to solve their problems.

But, if he'd gone searching for her, like the father of her child should, maybe her body would've been identified sooner despite the fact she'd been carrying Missy's wallet. Tristan would've grown up knowing his mother was never coming back. Also, maybe the Noëlville Serial Killer's investigation wouldn't have floundered and stalled the way it did. And then other people wouldn't have ended up terrified and freezing, wrapped in plastic the way he was now.

Maybe he'd have even let his own heart begin to heal from losing Lucy earlier. At least, he'd have begun to let go of the resentment that he'd held on to so tightly in his hand that he'd never begun to peel his fingers open to welcome someone new into his life.

But have you forgiven yourself?

The question he'd asked Gemma back by the lake filled his mind. She'd literally and physically disappeared and hidden from those who'd wanted to help her when she was in danger. He'd emotionally disappeared and shut his heart off so completely that no one had ever been able to find it.

Lord, forgive me for shutting myself off from those who You might've wanted to bring into my life. Help me forgive myself. Help me be the father Tristan needs me to be. Please, get me out of this mess, and when you do, open my heart to the life You want for me.

A chorus of barking filled his ears. Two dogs—no three— all howling and woofing at once as they charged through the snow toward him. Then the sound of men shouting filled his ears, and he saw the beams of flashlights moving outside his plastic cocoon.

"He's over here!" It was Jackson.

"Got him!" It was Caleb. "Patrick, can you hear me?"

He shouted as loudly as he could through his bonds, then felt three dogs pawing against the plastic and butting their heads against him. Relief moved through Patrick's core like a cleansing rain.

Thank You, Lord.
Thank You.

Moments later, they reached him. Patrick heard them call

to the dogs to stand down and watched as their silhouetted forms and flashlight beams moved above him in the darkness.

"Patrick." Finnick crouched down beside him. "Hang on. We're going to get you out of there."

Finnick, Caleb and Jackson fell into a focused near-silence as they worked together to free him, taking photos and collecting evidence as they went. Carefully, the plastic was cut away from his body, the duct tape was removed from his legs and chest and the gag was pulled from his mouth, and then Finnick reached for his hand. Patrick grabbed ahold of the inspector's outstretched hand and felt the older man haul him to his feet. Finnick pulled him into a firm and fatherly half hug. They were in a grouping of thick trees, no different than any patch of any number of forests in Northern Ontario. Only, this place could've been his grave. Caleb and Jackson were flanking him protectively, on either side. Simcoe, Jackson's K-9 partner, Hudson, and Finnick's black Labrador, Nippy, stood at attention just beyond them. Finnick made sure Patrick was stable on his feet before stepping back.

"You okay?" Finnick asked. Concern filled his eyes.

"Yeah," Patrick said, automatically.

Of course he was okay. He was always okay, right?

No, and Gemma had reminded him of the importance of saying so.

"Actually, I'm anything but okay," Patrick admitted. "I was terrified I was going to die out here, and I'm incredibly relieved to see you all, but I'm also incredibly worried that neither my son nor Gemma are here."

"We've lost them," Finnick said gently. "For now. But we're going to find them, and we're going to get them back. Come on. We'll explain on the walk back to the road."

The cops aimed their flashlights through the trees, and they started walking single file, with Finnick taking the lead and Jackson taking up the rear while Simcoe flanked Patrick protectively.

"As I'm sure Gemma told you, we got a call from Gabriel saying he had a lock on Missy and Tristan's location," Finnick started, after a long moment. So, Finnick's call to Gabriel's lawyer had worked.

"Unfortunately, Bone beat me to the rendezvous point," Jackson said. "When I got there, both Missy and Gabriel were dead, and Tristan was gone."

Patrick gasped a painful breath and felt Simcoe nudge him comfortingly. He reached down and ran his hand through Simcoe's fur.

"Blake has been coordinating with local provincial police on all of this," Finnick went on. "But unfortunately none of them were able to reach the trailer park in time so we were our own. We have security footage of the man you know as Bone walking Tristan to a car," Finnick said, "and ushering him inside. Your son seemed unharmed."

Patrick thanked God for that.

But now the hope of finding him seems even further away than ever.

"Then when I got to yours and Gemma's GPS location," Caleb added, picking up the story, "there was no one there. Just the broken snowmobile, the phones and signs of a struggle. But when I whistled, Simcoe ran out of the trees and practically leaped at me."

"Gemma told her to hide," Patrick said. He glanced down at the dog and whispered. "Good dog."

"From there it was just a matter of tracking you," Finnick said. "I can't tell you how relieved we were when Hudson was the one who found your scent first, and not Nippy."

Right, Nippy was a cadaver dog.

Patrick shivered to realize just how close he'd come to becoming the latest victim of the Noëlville Serial Killer. The trees parted ahead and they reached a rural stretch of road. There were two other trucks parked behind Jackson's, which Patrick guessed belonged to Caleb and Finnick.

"The OPP is continuing to push the Amber Alert," Finnick said. "And filter through leads from the public and look for Tristan."

Finnick leaned back against one of the trucks, and the other men stood in a circle around him.

"Here's what we've managed to piece together since our last team meeting," he went on. "We've been dealing with two competing parties, each with their own agendas. Basically, it looks like Missy has a long history of theft and criminal activity. According to Gabriel, years ago Missy and Lucy stole something from a party at Holly Jolly Ranch. But they crossed the wrong people, and some men in fedoras went after them—"

"Presumably, Rust, Bone and Umber," Caleb added. "This is why you should never steal from a serial killer—or in this case, three men handling the dirty work of someone very powerful."

"Yup," Finnick went on. "According to what Gabe told his lawyer, they got to Missy first. But she pointed all the blame at Lucy, told them that Lucy had robbed her too and planted her wallet on Lucy to bolster her story. So, they caught and killed Lucy."

Patrick blew out a long breath.

"Then recently, Missy managed to cross those same men again," Finnick said, "and ever since they've been after her to get the stash she stole back. She reached out to you and Tristan, pretending to be Lucy. But it was Tristan she was after. She sent gifts to butter him up and a game console to communicate with him behind your back. But Gabriel wasn't sure why."

"I'm guessing because she'd been banned from working the venue she wanted to rob," Patrick said, "and saw Tristan as her solution. She was going to use him for whatever her so-called last big job was."

His heart ached at the thought. Quickly, he filled them in on the Stroke of Midnight Room, and how both Lucy and Missy had been accused of stealing while on the job and had been banned from the premises.

"Chuck told me there's going to be a big event for children at Holly Jolly Ranch tonight," Patrick concluded. "They're supposed to be giving away thousands of expensive toys and electronics. Maybe while families are celebrating, some of the adults were planning on sneaking away to the Midnight Room for another kind of meeting. Gambling? Drugs? I don't know. For all we know, they're using children's events as a cover and have been for years."

But what did Missy steal and where was the stash now?

And if Rust, Bone and Umber were actually the Noëlville Serial Killer how were the Cold Case Task Force ever going to get the evidence they needed to prove it? And where were they holding Gemma and Tristan now?

"I got a couple of staff at Holly Jolly to talk to me off the record," Caleb said, "and everything you're saying matches what I got from them. Although they left out the part about a secret room where the cell phones won't work." He rolled his eyes. "Obviously there's going to be a major police investigation into the fact somebody opened fire at the ranch, and I'm sure Blake will keep us looped in as that unfolds. The facility's going to be getting lawyers for all the staff, to keep control of the flow of information. But the bottom line is yes, staff confirmed there's a big kids toy company who occasionally throws huge giveaway events. Sometimes they go for years without having one. Other times, they throw several in a year. It's dodgy."

"Which would match up with Patrick's theory that they were a cover for certain people to get together without raising suspicions," Jackson said and crossed his arms.

Caleb nodded. "Staff hate working the parties," he continued, "because there's always an exclusive side shindig for a small handful of mucky-mucks, who bring in their own security. They're held at odd times of the year and tend to bring in some outsiders to work indoor catering, who the regulars never see again. There were a lot of rumors and apparently 'the vibes felt really off.' But none of Holly Jolly's regular staff saw any proof of illegal activity."

"And if they're smart," Finnick said, "none of Holly Jolly's staff or the other guests will have any clue what the so-called mucky-mucks were up to. Which will make it very hard for police to get anything from interviewing them except hunches and innuendo. We still don't know Rust, Bone and Umber's true identities, let alone have proof they're the Noëlville Serial Killers. What's the name of the toy company?"

"LMNTL Enterprises, apparently." Caleb shrugged. "I'd never heard of it."

Sudden hope caught inside Patrick's chest.

"But I have!" Patrick turned and started for Jackson's truck, looking for Gemma's rucksack. "Missy sent Tristan an LMNTL game console to message Tristan with. What if she stole it from an LMNTL event? What if the killer was able to use it to track us to the diner and the cottage?"

And they would've kept using it to track them if Gemma hadn't had the quick thinking to create a Faraday cage around it. Well, maybe it cut both ways. He found the rucksack in the back seat of the car and carefully unwrapped Tristan's LMNTL game from the makeshift signal-blocking cage.

The task force stood around him as Patrick popped the batteries back in the console, hit the power button and the machine whirred to life. There was only one "friend" in the contact list. The name was listed only as M and presumably it was Missy.

"I'm hoping I'm right and they've hacked this feed," Patrick said. "A lot of companies can hack into their client's private conversations, even though they're not supposed to. Here's hoping LMNTL is one of those."

The chat box was open. Patrick prayed for guidance. Then he typed:

This is Tristan's father. I'm ready to negotiate.

The cursor blinked. Then slowly white letters appeared on the black screen.

Bring us the stash. You've got one hour. No cops. Just you.

Or your son and the woman die.

"Gemma! Gemma, wake up!"

A young and urgent voice was floating at the edges of Gemma's unconscious mind, trying to tug her back to reality. She couldn't place it. And yet, it was oddly familiar.

Her eyes fluttered open. Indistinct gray shapes filled her gaze. She closed her eyes again. Her mind was too heavy to think. Like someone had poured wet cement over her mental gears, stopping them from turning.

The last hour had been a disjointed string of confusing and terrifying moments.

One moment she'd been kissing Patrick, feeling safe in his arms. The next, pain was shooting through her body. When she'd woken up, she'd been sideways, uncomfortable and shaking, wedged bound and blindfolded in the back of some kind of vehicle. There'd been voices. She was terrified. Something damp and sickly sweet had been pressed over her face, and then she was sleeping again.

Patrick... Where's Patrick now?

Help me, Lord. I feel like my mind is drowning...

"Gemma!" The voice was almost shouting now. "Come on! I need your help!"

Her eyes snapped open, and this time she fought against letting the unconsciousness take hold.

Facts! Come on, Gemma. You're a private detective. Start gathering facts!

She opened her eyes, noting she was lying on a hard yet carpeted floor. Industrial carpet. She was probably in some kind of office building. The room was dark and windowless but not pitch-black. Faint electric light filtered through a crack under the door, and it was bright enough that her eyes should adjust if she was patient long enough. There was a cloth in her mouth, and her hands were tied behind her back with what felt like tape. But she wasn't tied overly tightly, and her feet weren't bound. So, presumably whoever had kidnapped her didn't think she was going to be that much trouble.

And she'd been kidnapped with someone. Somebody who needed her... Her gaze shifted to the boy huddled in the corner of the room.

"Tristan!" She sat up, joy flooding her heart, and forgetting for a moment that her mouth was gagged. The boy's name came out as a muffled mush of syllables. Her eyes strained to see into the darkness. "Tristan, is that you?"

"Yes!" The boy sounded excited, relieved and scared rolled

into one, as if he was clinging to the hope that they'd be able to escape now they were in this together.

She hoped so too.

Thank You, Lord. Please help me protect him and get him back to his father.

As her eyes kept adjusting to the darkness, she could now see they were locked in a plain-looking office, with bare walls, a tiled ceiling and a single door. Tristan was sitting cross-legged a few feet away from her, with his hands behind his back.

"They gagged my mouth too," Tristan said, "but I rubbed my cheeks on the floor and I was able to budge it down to my chin."

"Smart," she tried to say through her gag.

He'd sounded proud to have come up with a helpful idea, and considering everything they'd both gone through in the past several hours, her heart warmed to hear it. For a moment, she did the same with her gag, which made her think of the way Simcoe scratched her face on the floor when it was itchy. Finally, bit by bit, she eased it away from her mouth and past her chin. She gasped a deep breath, and felt clean air fill her lungs again.

"Okay!" she said, keeping her voice low in case there was anyone in the hall who might hear them. "That worked. Although, maybe we should keep our voices down in case there's someone outside the door."

"Sure." His voice dropped to a whisper. "Is my dad okay?"

Worry quivered in his voice, and yet there was a strength there too that made him so much like his dad. Her heart ached, wishing she could hug him and promise him everything would be okay.

Last time she'd seen Patrick, he'd been hit by a stun gun.

But she wasn't about to add that burden onto Tristan's already overladen heart.

"I think he's okay," she said. As she said the words she wrapped the hope of them around her like a cloak. "He's been really worried about you. Are you okay?"

"Yeah." Tristan's voice dropped slightly. "Nobody hurt me or anything."

She was relieved to hear it. "Do you want to talk about where you've been or what's been happening?" Gemma asked, gently.

"No," Tristan said. "Not really."

"Okay."

The responsibility of protecting and caring for this kid weighed heavily on her heart.

Lord, give me the patience to wait until he's ready. Guide me and show me how to take care of him, and get us both out of here.

She heard Tristan swallow hard. "Okay, now what do we do next?" he asked. He sounded every bit as hopeful as he had when he'd expected her to chase after the men who'd kidnapped his dad the day before.

There was something about Tristan that got to her. Something that made her want to help him. To not let Tristan down.

And to live up to being the person that this kid thought she could be.

She wondered if that was how Patrick must feel being his father. Her jaw rose. She would do everything in her power to get Tristan back to Patrick. No matter what it took. She'd find a way to save both of their lives. Either way, she was always better trying to focus on practical and tangible problems than just sitting doing nothing but worry.

"How about we move back-to-back, so I can feel how your hands are tied?" she suggested.

"Okay," Tristan agreed.

It took some work to shuffle across the room toward each other. But finally she and the boy were back-to-back, leaning against each other like the inverse of a hug. She felt for his wrists. They were bound with tape, not plastic zip ties. Better yet, they were bound over the sleeves of a flannel shirt, which was so oversize she suspected it was Patrick's. There was hope that with enough time and hard enough work they'd be able to work free. She dug her nails into the tape and started scratching at it.

She'd learned as a private detective that sometimes the best way to get someone to open up about something they didn't want to talk about was just to start telling stories yourself—let the other person know that it was okay to talk—and be patient.

"So, do you remember asking me about whether I had a boat?" she started, keeping her voice light. "When the bad guys showed up at my cottage, we decided to escape across the lake in the boat."

"Really?" Tristan leaned forward. "But you said the lake was kind of frozen."

"It was!" Gemma said. "But your dad broke the ice up with an axe."

Tristan snorted. She kept going, skipping over the surface of the story and focusing on the parts he might find funny, to protect Tristan's mind from sinking down into fear.

"Then we found this barn to camp out in overnight," she said. "My brother, Jackson, showed up with his German shepherd. But Patrick didn't recognize him at first, so he tried to fight him."

"Ha!" A laugh exploded through Tristan's lungs. It was loud and spontaneous, and warmed Gemma's heart. "My dad would totally do that."

"Your dad is pretty amazing," Gemma said. "He's the best."

"I know," Tristan said.

She kept working at the duct tape, peeling it away, one fraction of an inch at a time. And slowly, Tristan began to tell his story.

To hear the kid tell it—the whole thing had started with one little lie that had continued to snowball out of control.

"Dad says I'm not allowed to talk with strangers online in my games," Tristan said. "But all the best games involve playing with other people. So, I figured out how to hack his password and turn off the parental controls on my old game system. Then Missy sent me a friend request. She kept giving me online coins, upgrades and downloads that made the game better." He sighed. "I just wanted to play cooler games with better characters, like the other kids I know."

"I get that," Gemma said.

"She told me that she was my mom, and she was so nice… I wanted it to be true," Tristan said. "I know now that she isn't, because Gabriel told me and showed me pictures of them with my mom from before." He paused, and his voice cracked a bit as he added, "I know now that my real mom's dead." Gemma's heart broke for the boy as he wiped his nose on his sleeve. "I wanted Missy to be my mom," he continued. "Because I wanted a mom, like everyone else. And Dad would never tell me anything about Mom. He always just shut me down. Missy told me she'd asked Dad to let her be in my life and he'd said no. She told me that she'd been sending me presents, but that Dad wouldn't let me have them either. Why would he do that?"

"You'll have to ask your dad about that," Gemma said. She peeled a long piece of duct tape off with a satisfying scratching sound. "But yes, I know his top priority is protecting you.

Tristan... I'm so sorry about your mom." She wished she could take his pain away. When all this was over, she hoped Patrick would call Teresa—the boy had a lot to process.

"Thanks," he said. Tristan went on to explain how he'd gotten Missy to send the new LMNTL game system by courier on a day he knew his dad wouldn't be home. Then when they were in the diner, he'd gotten a message from Missy that she was outside, and he'd gone to meet her.

"But then everything spun out of control," he said. His words flew out in one big rush.

"I was standing out back looking for her, and this guy in a hat ran up and shot a gun. He said he was shooting at a bear, but I thought he was shooting at my mom. I saw her run away and knew she was okay, and I didn't know what to tell Dad, because he didn't know about the game. Then my dad was kidnapped, we got him back, and then Missy showed up outside the cottage and begged me to let her explain before I told Dad. So, I climbed out the window to talk to her, because I didn't know what else to do. And she kind of kidnapped me. But I didn't realize she'd kidnapped me at first. Or maybe I did and didn't want to admit it. I don't know."

The tape finally yanked free. She turned back to see Tristan scrambling to his feet. Then he threw his arm around her neck and hugged her tightly. Through tears he babbled something about a man in a fedora taking him away from Missy and Gabriel, hearing gunshots and knowing they were dead and waking up here.

"I was alone," he said, "and I was terrified. Then they opened the door and threw you in, and I knew it was going to be okay."

Tears flooded her eyes and streamed down her cheeks. Her arms ached to hug him back. She took a good scan of him head to toe, and he seemed relatively unharmed, physically.

Lord, it feels wrong that a child this young has had to face so much pain and fear. Guard his heart. Help him heal. And help me get him safely back to his dad.

"It's okay," she said. "I'm here now. Your hands are free. You're going to get my hands free. Then we'll get out of here and get you back to your dad."

Tristan let her go and pulled back. "You promise?"

"I promise I will do everything in my power to make it happen." And she would.

He wiped his eyes. "Okay."

Then Tristan moved around behind her and made quick work of ripping the tape off her wrists.

Time for the next task—escape.

She checked her pockets and instructed Tristan to do the same. As expected, they were empty. She'd lost her phone, her keys and anything she might possibly use as a weapon. There was also no furniture in the room. The doorknob didn't move, and there was no perceivable way to remove either it or the door hinges. There was a light switch though and a domed light on the ceiling.

Tristan reached for the switch.

"Stop." She grabbed his hand right before his fingers could make contact. "Someone might see the light under the door, and we don't want them to know we've gotten free. I'm going to hoist you up onto my shoulders to check the light. We might be able to pry one of the brackets off and use it to remove the door hinges."

"Cool," Tristan said.

She walked over to the far wall and cupped her hands like a step for Tristan. He planted his feet in them, and she hoisted him up. He scrambled up onto her shoulders, walking his hands up the wall for support, and then reached for the ceiling. She heard a thud.

"Hey, the ceiling tiles move!" he said. There were more thuds, then the sound of two panels sliding against each other. "It's a drop ceiling!"

His weight disappeared from her shoulders. She looked up and saw nothing but an empty hole where one of the tiles had been.

"Wait!" she said. "Where did you go?"

"Into the ceiling!" Tristan said. His head dropped upside down through the hole. His mop of blond hair fell down around his face. "There's a space up here above the tiles. They're suspended on a grid. Dad showed me how they install them. You can climb up and then we can get into the vents or just stick to support beams and crawl above the ceiling." Then he frowned as if seeing the obvious problem. "Oh, right, you've got nothing to climb on. Hang on."

Tristan's head disappeared again. She heard him moving around inside the ceiling.

And was it her imagination or was there the sound of footsteps coming from the other side of the door? Following this kid through a hole in the ceiling might be one of the most ridiculous things she'd ever done, but it wasn't like there were a lot of other options.

Then she saw one sleeve of the plaid shirt dangling down through the hole.

"Come on!" Tristan said. "You can use it to climb up. I tied it to a girder. Dad showed me how. I'm really good at knots. Trust me."

Thank You Lord, for Tristan's courage and initiative, and that Patrick was such a caring father who taught his son the family business. Our lives are in Your hands. I'll follow whatever way You guide me to get this boy to safety.

Even if it means climbing into the ceiling and slithering through the air vents. The footsteps outside the door sounded closer. She leaped up, grabbed the cuff of the shirt and wrapped her hand around it. It lurched a little under her weight, but Tristan's knot held. She braced her feet against the wall and climbed up.

Then she felt Tristan's hands grab ahold of her wrists and help her up.

"You've got to be careful around the tiles," Tristan said, "because they break into pieces really easily."

She crawled through the hole and followed the soles of Tristan's shoes through a narrow gap and into a metal vent. He reached back, untied the shirt and pulled it through the hole and slid the panel back.

"Alright," Tristan said, "now all we've got to do is climb through the vents until we find a way out."

She couldn't see his face in the darkness, but he sounded almost excited at the prospect. He started to crawl and she followed.

Not that she had any idea where they were going or how long it would be until their captors figured out they were gone. But they were free and out of the room, and she'd tackle one problem at a time.

"I've never been allowed to crawl through vents before," Tristan added. "Dad just let me stick my head in. So, this is fun. Well, I mean it's not totally fun. But Dad always said panicking doesn't help anything."

"Yeah, that sounds like him."

And her heart longed with the hope that they'd both see Patrick again soon.

For several long and agonizing moments, they crawled through the dark metal air vents, randomly choosing between forks in their path, squeezing around uncomfortably angled corners and pausing whenever shouts and footsteps reached their ears. There were men moving around the building now.

And judging by the volume of shouted swear words and the slamming doors, they'd realized Gemma and Tristan were gone. No doubt, the men would be hunting for them. She just hoped they wouldn't check the vents. They needed to find a safe place to drop down and exit the building.

Suddenly, Tristan stopped.

"What's up?" she asked.

"We've hit a dead end," Tristan said. Worry flooded his voice, as if the hope he'd been holding on to had suddenly started slipping away. "It's a concrete wall. I'm guessing we hit the edge of the building."

"Alright," she said, keeping her voice positive. "That just means we find a new way out. There was really chilly air coming from the last fork we passed. Maybe it leads to the roof."

She slid her body backward on the next vent exit, slid her torso out into the empty space above a new drop ceiling and pushed back a tile. She waited for her eyes to adjust to the darkness. It was some kind of warehouse office room, with pallets of boxes and computers behind small metal desks. Artificial light filtered in from under a doorway, but the room was empty. She steeled a breath. Computers and electricity meant they might have a connection to the internet, which they could use to call for help. She dropped down and landed softly on the floor below. By the time she'd turned back to tell Tristan to stay hidden in the vents, he'd already jumped through.

Carefully, she crept to the door and looked out into the hallway. Voices filtered down the hall to her right. An exit lay to her left, with signs that opening it would trigger an emergency alarm. She slipped back inside, closed the door and locked it behind her.

"Okay," she said, "Good news is we've got an exit. Bad

news is I need to try to disable the lock and switch off the alarm system or we'll be trapped at the dead end of a hallway with loud sirens telling the bad guys where to find us."

Gemma sat down in a seat behind the closest computer.

"Will do." Tristan ran over to the door. "Try 12345 as the password. It's what Dad always uses."

Gemma made a mental note to tell Patrick to change his password when they got out.

Then she switched on the machine. A quick search of the desk turned up an orange sticky note with a string of letters and numbers. She typed them into a prompt box and the machine purred to life. So far so good. The logo for LMNTL Enterprises filled the screen. They'd been kidnapped by killers working for a kids game company?

A few moments later she'd found the security system and hit another password block. This one wasn't so easy to crack, but it also didn't have any mechanism that locked a person out after guessing the password wrong too many times. So, she created a quick alphanumeric hacking mechanism to scroll through possible passwords for her. Then she tried to get online and hit another snag—the password that had logged her into the machine didn't seem to get her onto the internet. Either that or the server was down because of the storm. She glanced over to Tristan who was checking out the shelves of what looked like toy prototypes.

"Come here," she called, quietly, and waved him over. "I need backup."

Tristan nodded and ran over.

"I can't get online. I'm going to run a diagnostic. I want you to look around the desks and see if you can find another sticky note like this one." The kid flashed her an endearing smile and a thumbs-up. Then he started searching. The password hacking program kept whirring through numbers.

Now, there was nothing to do but help Tristan search for the password or wait for the computer to figure it out.

Or, she could take the opportunity to find the evidence she needed on Rust, Umber and Bone, solve the murders and put them away for good.

She'd always been good at researching. Could the information she needed to finally solve the murders really be here at her fingertips?

A few keystrokes later and she'd opened a file directory. Inventory, expenses, shipments. Nothing that indicated crime. She clicked on Personnel. A huge database opened. LMNTL had over twenty thousand employees, who could be searched by name, income, location, projects and role. But she needed more. She opened a programming window and searched for any personal info that might be hidden from view. A moment later hope brushed her spine. There was a hidden log line labeled Expenses. Now to see if any LMNTL employees had charged very expensive wool coats and fedoras to the company card.

With shaking fingers, she created the search parameters and hit Enter. A second later, three names appeared along with company identification photos: Steve Waddington, Bob Bruwer and Harry Manahan, aka Rust, Umber and Bone. All three had been working for LMNTL for over fifteen years and were classified as Special Project. Her chest tightened. "Quick, I need a thumb drive!"

"Got it." Tristan appeared at her side with a small red drive he must've found in a drawer. She plugged it into the computer and started copying files into it as quickly as she could. There were the men's full names, dates of birth and social security numbers. All three had a list of projects for which they'd received bonuses between twenty and forty thousand dollars each. A deeper dive into hidden subdirectories and she'd found what each of those "special projects" had been—victims of the Noëlville Serial Killers. The freelance tax accountant and the lawyer had been killed for uncovering some of the board members' financial irregularities. The contractor, the dishwasher and one of the caterers had been murdered for witnessing a board member's impropriety. Three others, including Lucy and Missy, had lost their lives for theft. But that wasn't all. There were almost a dozen more names, all with bounties attached to them. Were these victims who'd escaped their death, as Oscar had theorized? Or were there more victims out there waiting to be found?

Her fingers flew as she wrote down each name along with all the details she could find.

The computer dinged, and then it was like she could hear the faint sound of dozens of switches going off around the building. Her code had worked. The alarms had been disabled and the doors had been unlocked.

She grabbed the thumb drive from the back of the computer and clenched it tightly. "Let's go."

Together they ran for the door. She pushed it open. Voices were shouting now somewhere beyond her field of vision, but the hallway and they had a clear path to the door.

Thank You, God.

They ran down the hallway, as quietly as they could. The door lay in front of them. She pushed it open, cool air brushed her face, then the door stopped suddenly and she heard the loud jangle of chains. Disappointment surged through her. "It's locked from the outside."

The door was ajar now, but only a few inches.

"Let me try," Tristan said. "I might be able to squeeze out and then unlock it from the outside."

It was worth a go. Tristan held his breath and squeezed his skinny frame into the gap. For a moment, he grunted in pain and she was afraid he was stuck, then suddenly he yanked himself free and disappeared through the hole.

"I'm out!" Tristan's hopeful face looked back at her through the gap.

Suddenly, she heard loud footsteps barreling down the hallway toward her and heard Rust's voice swear.

They'd been found!

She tried in vain to squeeze herself through the gap sideways, only to felt her shoulders and hips wedge hard against the frame. "Quick!" She shoved the thumb drive toward Tristan's hands. "Take this and run. Find somewhere safe to hide. Don't look back. I'll be okay!"

Tristan hesitated. "Are you sure?"

"I had faith we'd find you. You've got to help me by holding onto that faith too. Now go!"

Tristan hesitated again. Then he snatched the thumb drive and ran off into the night. She pulled her arm back through the door and it closed behind her. The man she'd known as Rust charged down the hall toward her. His face was red in anger as he aimed the gun between her eyes. Instinctively, her hands rose.

"Enough games!" he shouted. "You're coming with me and we're going to end this."

THIRTEEN

The Sudbury morning fog was so thick that Patrick could barely see the ugly box-shaped industrial building in front of him, let alone any sign of the police backup that was hiding just outside his field of view.

He took a deep breath, prayed for God's protection and walked alone toward the ugly yellow lights cutting through the gloom. In his hands, he clutched a large box filled with fake and dye-packed cash, which he hoped would pass for the mysterious "stash" he'd agreed to trade his son's and Gemma's lives for. A bulletproof vest lay under his jacket. A hidden earpiece connected him to the team he couldn't see.

No matter how alone he looked and felt, he wasn't alone anymore. And he had hope that together they'd get his son and Gemma back safely.

After Patrick had made contact with the killers via Tristan's LMNTL game device, Jackson had pointed out that their greatest advantage might be the fact that Rust, Umber and Bone probably had no idea Patrick was working with police.

Their biggest disadvantage was that they'd had barely an hour to assemble backup and mount a rescue operation.

"Your job is just to walk up to that door," Jackson's voice was in his ear, "wait for the bad guys to open it and then let us take over from there. I don't want you rushing into danger."

Patrick's jaw clenched. "Got it."

"Look, I've never been up against a trio of serial killers like this before," Gemma's brother added, "but I spent some time in juvenile detention as a kid and dealt with my fair share of bullies. At the end of the day, Rust, Umber and Bone are bullies. They work security for a big company, get paid a lot of money and, as the expression goes, these guys are always punching down. Catering staff, freelance contractors and dishwashers—they've been tasked with targeting people they think can't stand up to them. They are used to being told to go after people working to make ends meet. They probably saw your company's name on the side of your van and thought they could push you around like every other little guy they've pushed around. They have no idea you've got a veritable army of help behind you."

Finnick, Jackson, Caleb and Lucas of the Cold Case Task Force were now positioned like a clock in a circle around him somewhere in the fog. Beyond them, on side streets, hid a fleet of Ontario Provincial Police officers, waiting for Blake to give them the signal from the task force to move in. But Patrick could see none of them as he walked toward the building. Thick, wet fog enveloped his body. The sound of his own footsteps squelching on a badly plowed parking lot filled his ears.

Thank You for my backup, Lord. Even when I can't see them. And I know I've got You surrounding me, Lord. You've always been there, even when I've pushed You away and tried to make my own way. Thank You for everyone You've sent to help me. Please help us get Tristan and Gemma out safe.

"We've got movement!" Caleb's voice crackled in his ear. "Someone is running through the trees toward Patrick!"

A second later he saw the lanky silhouette appearing in the gloom, and his heart knew it in a glance.

"It's Tristan!" he yelled. He sprinted through the gray toward his son. Hope exploded in his chest. "Tristan!"

"Dad!" His son's voice broke.

A second later and Patrick reached him. He bent down and opened his arms wide as Tristan launched himself into his chest so hard it knocked Patrick back on his heels. For a long moment, he hugged his son tightly and his son hugged him back just as fiercely, as a mixture of laughter, tears and prayers of relief filled Patrick's heart.

Then Tristan pushed back, and Patrick let him go.

"You've got to go rescue Gemma," Tristan said, earnestly. "She's in there, and she saved my life, so I could escape."

"You saw her?" Finnick asked, emerging from the fog to Patrick's right with Nippy and Simcoe. Patrick hadn't even realized the head of the Cold Case Task Force was walking his way until suddenly he was there. Simcoe wagged her tail and butted her head against Patrick's legs.

Tristan turned to Finnick.

"Yes, sir," Tristan said. He fished a red thumb drive from his pocket and handed it to the inspector. "She said to give you this. It has the bad men's real names and identities, and information about the people they killed, even ones she says you don't know about. She hacked into a computer."

"Of course she did." Finnick whistled softly as he took the paper. "Gemma is unbelievable and so are you, kid. You're a real hero, just like your dad."

Tristan beamed and Patrick felt a lump form in his throat.

"She unlocked the doors too," Tristan added, "and disarmed the security system."

"That could be helpful," Finnick said, "unless someone managed to rearm them." He turned to Patrick. "Take your son to the safe zone back behind the police vehicles. We'll get another member of the team to go in and retrieve Gemma."

"But you're going to go in the building and get her, right, Dad?" Tristan looked up at his father. "Gemma is the absolute best."

"You're right," he admitted. "Gemma is...the absolute best."

"She helped me escape." Tristan said. "She saved your life, she saved mine and now it's our turn to save her, right?"

Something lurched in Patrick's heart as he looked down at his son's earnest face.

In ways he couldn't begin to put into words. Did Tristan have any idea just how much he wanted to burst into that building, find Gemma and rescue her? Even if it meant risking his own life? Even if it meant battling a dozen killers or more?

"You're the Fire Chief and the Head of Search and Rescue," Tristan argued. "You know how to save people."

"But I'm not a cop," Patrick said. "I don't have a gun or a badge."

Although, if the team did decide they wanted a flashy distraction, he was the guy for the job. He knew enough from on-the-job experience how fires started, though he wouldn't do that here...but he also knew how to rig a small explosive.

Tristan closed his eyes for a moment, and Patrick knew he was praying. He silently thanked God for the young man his son was growing up to be. Then Tristan opened his eyes and looked up at his dad again.

"You want to go help rescue her, don't you?" Tristan asked. "You don't want to go to a safe zone. You want to help Gemma, because you know that if either of us were in trouble she wouldn't let her boss or team tell her she couldn't help us." Patrick exhaled. Tristan was right. He turned to Finnick. The inspector was chuckling softly under his breath, and for a moment a look glimmered in his eyes that made Patrick suspect he was thinking about his own fiancée, Casey.

"Kid's right," Patrick said. He pulled Tristan to his side and gave him a half hug. "And I don't know what kind of lesson I'm going to be teaching my son if I go back to the safe zone, when everything in my core is telling me to run into the building."

"Tristan's out and I'm grateful, but they may be more desperate now." Finnick ran his hand over the back of his head. "I can't send a civilian in now. Not without a really good reason."

"How about the fact that they asked for me specifically and I'm the person they're planning on seeing?" Patrick said. "I'll take the box in. Caleb and Jackson can cover me."

"I hear you," Finnick said. "I will take Tristan behind the safe zone and make sure the lad stays put. You take the box of funny money to the door. Jackson and Caleb will have your back. You are not to get involved in the action. You hear me? No heroics."

"No heroics," Patrick echoed, only to feel the tell-tale prickling at the back of his heart that told him there was something he might be missing that God wanted him to see.

He closed his eyes and prayed silently.

Unless You, Father God, are telling me something different. You have been my Light in every dark and smokey room, guiding me when I couldn't see.

What would You have me do?

"I'm concerned we might be walking into a trap," Jackson's voice crackled in his ear. "Now that Tristan's escaped, they're going to be keeping a pretty close eye on Gemma. If police burst in, they'll probably shoot her before we can reach her. We need to find a way to create a smokescreen and put distance between the killers before we can risk sending police in."

Then Patrick opened his eyes again. "I have an idea."

***

Gemma was tied to a plain metal chair in the middle of the largest warehouse she'd ever seen in her life. Labyrinthian conveyor belts and towering boxes of expensive toys surrounded her on all sides. Bone and Rust flanked her with their guns raised and their faces red with anger.

And despite the fear that filled her body, she could feel another equally powerful emotion stirring inside her too—gratitude. She closed her eyes to the killers in front of her and prayed.

Thank You Lord that Tristan escaped. Please, please keep him safe.

"Look at me!" Bone demanded.

No, she was talking to someone far more important than these killers right now.

Then suddenly and without warning, Bone and Umber opened fire. The terrifying wave of sound overwhelmed her. A scream tore from somewhere deep inside her chest. She was surrounded and helpless, tied to a chair in an unknown building and being flanked by men who were now firing their guns so close to her body she could practically feel them whizzing past. She heard the bullets tearing through the cardboard boxes behind her and ricocheting off metal.

Help me, God! You promise that Your peace surpasses all understanding. But right now, I'm helpless, I'm terrified and all I feel is fear.

Then it hit her. What they were doing to her right now, firing around like this, was just another scare tactic from a group of killers who'd been using fear to terrorize people since the beginning. And sure, this was a downright terrifying and effective approach that was definitely working. But this time, she could acknowledge the fear, without letting it overwhelm her. This time, she would not let the fear win.

Her eyes snapped open.

"Alright, I'm scared!" she shouted at the top of her lungs. "I get that you're trying to scare me, and it's working. You did it. I'm really, really terrified!"

The hail of bullets petered off. Whatever these shooters had been expecting, it hadn't been that. The men in expensive fedoras and coats stared at her with the cold, dead and lifeless eyes of men who'd killed so many times they'd lost their connection to their own humanity.

Umber appeared behind them in a doorway, and she realized that not only did he still have a large white bandage on his nose from where Patrick had walloped him with her canoe paddle, he also had black eyes forming on either side. Bone seemed to be limping a bit too, and Rust was cradling the arm that Simcoe had bit.

You might be terrifying monsters. But you're still human. And one way or the other, we're going to beat you.

Then, another figure stepped in front of Umber.

He. Had. Patrick.

Fresh fear filled her heart as she watched Patrick step slowly into the room, with his chin raised and a large cardboard box in his hand. Umber followed him closely, with the gun pointed to his head. Patrick's warm and protective eyes locked on her face.

"It's going to be okay," he called to her. "Tristan is safe. Thank you for saving my s—"

—son.

The word was swallowed up by a groan as Umber smacked him hard across the back of the head. The box fell from Patrick's hands and fell to the ground on its side, where it lay on the concrete floor inches from her feet. The flap came open. Packets of hundred dollar bills spilled out.

"What's this?" Umber snarled and then swore. He looked at her. "Where's the stash?"

Suddenly, despite the fear, she felt like laughing.

"I still have no idea what the stash *is*," she admitted. "I never did and I don't care. All this time you've been chasing someone who stole something from some party. But you've been wrong from the beginning. I'm not a thief. I'm a private detective trying to solve the death of an amazing kid's mother, and I've got the best and strongest team of people in the world behind me."

She could hear her voice quivering, but she locked her eyes on Patrick. And let herself absorb all the strength, courage, care and pride she could feel in his gaze. A faint smile crossed his lips.

Keep going, he mouthed. *Don't stop.*

He wanted her to keep talking? Was this part of a plan?

Either way, she had more than enough she wanted to say to the men who'd been hunting and terrorizing them.

"You think you've been hunting me, Steve, Harry and Bob?" Gemma asked. "Well, all this time you're the ones who've been hunted. The police know your real names and identities. They know LMNTL has been using you to do their dirty work and cover up their ugly deeds to maintain the toy company's squeaky-clean image. And that for over a decade the three of you have been killing people, wrapping them in plastic and dumping them in the woods to let people think the Noëlville Serial Killer is real.

"So, yeah, you can terrify me. You can even kill me. But all you've got is fear and you've already lost."

A cold and petrifying silence spread between the men. Gemma watched as their eyes narrowed. She heard Umber load a bullet into the gun and didn't know if it was intended for her or Partrick. Either way, she knew he was planning for somebody's life to end. She felt her chin begin to quiver and prayed to God for help.

Then suddenly the cardboard box exploded into a cloud of thick smoke and hundred-dollar bills. Her chair flew backwards from the force of the explosion, and the killers and their weapons disappeared from her eyes. Their vile threats and profanity filled the air. She pitched backward and fell, bracing herself for the inevitable impact of the back smacking hard against the ground. Instead, she saw Patrick leap for her through the smoke and felt his strong arms wrap around her protectively and gently brought her to the ground.

"It's okay," Patrick's voice whispered in her ear, even as she felt him cutting her loose from the chair. "I've got you."

She rolled out of the chair onto the cold concrete onto her hands and knees. Patrick grabbed her hand and quickly pulled her behind a metal conveyor belt.

"Hi." Patrick's voice was low and husky. Joy filled his dark eyes and everything inside her wanted to throw her arms around him and hold him tight. "Escape now. Hug later."

Then he raised a police walkie-talkie to his lips.

"I've got her," Patrick said. "Time to finish this."

FOURTEEN

Chaos exploded around Patrick, with dozens of authoritative voices shouting and thick white smoke billowing in from either side. He grabbed hold of Gemma's hand and felt her squeeze him back. He saw the glowing red letters of the Exit sign, and together they ran for it, as Caleb and Jackson burst in, flanked by dozens of uniformed OPP officers. He heard police telling the three killers to get down on the ground and drop their guns.

Within a moment, police officers were flanking them and directing them to safety. They ran out the emergency exit into the crisp morning air. The fog was beginning to clear. The first few rays of the morning sun were beginning to spread across the snow.

Behind him he could hear Umber, Bone and Rust shouting nonsense threats to the police arresting them, as officers put them in handcuffs and read them their rights. But he wasn't even tempted to turn and look back. Everything he needed was either by his side or lay ahead of him. He slid his hand from Gemma's and wrapped his arm around her shoulder, pulling her even closer to his side. She slid her hand around his waist and nestled herself against him. They kept running forward toward the yellow tape that police had set up to cordon off the scene. In moments he saw Jackson and Hudson coming toward them from their right. Jackson lifted the tape. Patrick and Gemma ran through. Jackson and his K-9 followed.

Then he saw Tristan charging like a torpedo through the snow with Simcoe by his side, and Finnick and Nippy one step behind.

Patrick and Gemma pulled apart as Tristan reached them. But Tristan wrapped his arms around them both and hugged them tightly.

Patrick ran his hand down the back of his son's head as Tristan buried his face in his side.

"See, Dad, I told you that you could do it!"

"You did," Patrick said, feeling thick and happy tears choke his throat. "And you were right. But to be fair, it was Jackson who said we needed to create a smoke screen to get you away from the killers."

"Yeah, but I didn't mean literally!" Jackson guffawed and threw his arms around Gemma in an embrace so wide that his fingers reached to include Patrick and Tristan too.

"What can I say?" Patrick laughed. "I know a lot about making smoke and charging through it!"

Then Finnick was slapping his hand on Patrick's back, and Simcoe, Hudson and Nippy were butting into the hugs as well, wagging their tails and pawing at Patrick's legs.

"This is Sergeant Murphy." Blake's voice suddenly crackled through all their radios at once. "I need Inspector Ethan Finnick and the Cold Case Task Force to meet me at the far edge of the perimeter immediately."

Finnick stepped back, and Patrick watched as the inspector met Gemma's eye. She shrugged. The team jogged toward the edge of the perimeter. He saw Lucas and his yellow Lab, Michigan, emerge from the trees to his left. Then Caleb jogged toward them. Sergeant Blake Murphy was in full Ontario Provincial Police uniform, with her long black hair tied back under her hat.

"Finnick." She turned to the inspector. "The OPP is taking over jurisdiction of this crime scene. The emergency response team has the situation under control, the suspects in custody and is already using the information that your team has provided to get both arrest warrants and search warrants for the LMNTL corporation. I'm ordering you and your team to leave this scene immediately."

"Are you now?" Finnick's lips quirked. "Under whose authority?"

"Your fiancée, Casey," Blake said, and grinned. "She's expecting you at the altar in two hours, and with current traffic you're cutting it close. She's told me to remind you not to speed."

Finnick roared in laughter. Then he looked around at his team.

"Okay," he said. "I can't argue with that, especially as I have full faith in Blake to manage things here."

"You can all head to my house to freshen up," Patrick said. "I've got coffee, hot water and a couple of half-decent suits if you guys want to raid my wardrobe." He glanced at Gemma and shrugged. "I'm not sure what I have that'll fit you, but you're welcome to anything you can find."

She chuckled softly, and he found himself thinking he could quite happily hear her laugh every day for the rest of his life. "I'll figure something out."

"Okay, so it's decided," Finnick said. His jaw set and his blue eyes sparkled. "We head to Patrick's, get turned around and try our very best to make it to the church on time."

"I'll let Casey know to meet you at the altar," Blake said, then she turned to Jackson. "Amy and Skye are with Casey and her son now and will meet you there too." Her smile widened. "Safe travels."

They split into vehicles and drove up to Manitoulin Island single file. As much as Patrick wanted to ride with Gemma, she and Simcoe quickly slipped into her brother's truck, and she suggested that he and Tristan travel with Lucas and his K-9, Michigan.

He guessed that Gemma had wanted to give him and Tristan time alone to talk. Maybe she'd even known that having Michigan's youthful K-9 energy in the car would help Tristan relax and make him feel more comfortable opening up. If so, she was right, as his son talked to him nonstop for the entire drive back to the island. Tristan poured out the entire story from the beginning, about how he'd enabled online chat on his old gaming device when he knew he wasn't allowed to, how he'd become friends with Missy and she'd started sending him online money for upgrades, before eventually luring him to meet her.

"I knew it was bad," Tristan said, "but I didn't know how to tell you without admitting everything, getting in trouble and losing my game. Am I losing my game?"

"You're losing all your gaming privileges for quite a while," Patrick said, "and then not getting them back until I've some strong parental controls in place. But there are a lot of fun things we can do that aren't on computers."

"And you forgive me?"

"Of course," Patrick said. "I will always, always forgive you. No matter what."

Still, he found he needed to tell Tristan that he was forgiven several times on the drive home. And maybe he'd need to spend the rest of his life reminding and reassuring him. But that was the job of being Dad. And it was one he was thankful for. Even if the events of the past couple of days had reminded him that maybe he didn't need to do it alone. Gemma had recommended a therapist who provided counselling to kids who'd been through rough things. And he could get better at relying on friends and family too.

The conversation turned to Lucy—it broke his heart that Tristan had found out about her death from Gabriel instead of his own dad. Patrick made mistakes...maybe he should've talked about her more, but it wasn't too late, and maybe he needed to forgive himself too.

When they got to the house, Lucas and Tristan took all the K-9s for a run around the block, so the dogs would get some exercise in before being expected to sit still through the wedding, while the other members of the team split into different rooms to get ready for the wedding. Patrick made coffee and laid out some stuff to make sandwiches.

He was standing alone in his living room beside the Christmas tree when he heard the unmistakable sound of Gemma's footsteps on the floor behind him.

"What do you think?" she asked.

He turned and met her eyes. His mouth went dry. She was wearing one of his bright blue button-up shirts as a dress, over a simple black tank top and leggings, which he recognized from the contents of her rucksack. The hem of the shirt brushed her knees. She'd rolled the sleeves of the shirt up past her elbows and had run a brush through her hair, sending gentle wisps falling down around her face. And he knew without a doubt he'd never seen anything more beautiful in his life.

"You look incredible," he admitted. His voice sounded husky to his own ears. "But you sure you wouldn't prefer a dress? I'm sure we can borrow from somewhere?"

"Thanks, but I like this."

"I really like it too." He opened his arms and reached for her. She stepped into his embrace, and he hugged her deeply.

"You have a beautiful home," she said. "I love all the windows and wood."

"Thanks," he said. "I built it myself."

"Yeah, you told me," she said. Gemma pulled back, just enough to look up into his eyes. But still he didn't let go of her and she didn't let go of him. "And I want you to know that I really respect the fact you built a home and life here for your son, along with a business and reputation that people clearly respect. I can see why you don't want to leave it to move to the city."

"And your team is incredible," Patrick said. "I can see why you'd never want to leave them."

For a moment he stood there, staring at her and wishing he could find the words to tell her just how amazing he thought she was, how thankful he was that she was standing there in his living room and how he wished there was some way he could rearrange the world so that his life and hers lined up together.

Or was that just an obstacle they were both throwing up to keep from facing the fear of falling in love?

Love was scary. It meant opening his heart up and risking getting it trampled again.

Cheerful voices sounded on the steps outside. Tristan, Lucas and the dogs were back. Gemma stood up on her tiptoes and brushed a kiss across Patrick's lips. Then before he could kiss her back, she pulled away, just as the front door opened.

"Three K-9s walked and ready to go!" Lucas called.

"And it's time to get out of here and head to the church," Finnick said. The inspector walked out of the back room in a black tux and bow tie. Then he knelt down and fastened a matching bow tie around Nippy's neck.

Simcoe barked sharply. Finnick straightened up suddenly.

The team turned. The fur had risen at the back of Simcoe's neck, and the dog was sniffing around the living room.

"She senses something," Gemma said. She crouched down beside the dog. "Show me."

"I can't imagine what it could be," Patrick said.

For a moment, they all watched as the kelpie paced the living room. Her tan and brown snout sniffed the air. Then she walked over to the garage door, pawed at it and woofed loudly. Patrick opened the door and switched the light on. She made a beeline for a black tarp in the corner.

"What's under there?" Finnick asked, and concern cut through his voice.

"Just the gifts that Missy sent Tristan," Patrick said. "I'd completely forgotten that she'd apparently wanted one of them back. But I opened them all, and there was nothing suspicious in them."

"Clearly, Simcoe doesn't think so," Gemma said. She pulled the tarp back. Simcoe made a beeline for a punching bag. The K-9 sat in front of it. "Anybody got a knife?"

Silently, Patrick pulled a construction knife off his tool bench and handed it to her. She dug it deeply into the punching bag and sliced. White powder poured out. She leaped back and called Simcoe to her side.

Caleb whistled. "Well, that looks like a pretty big stash to me."

"What are we looking at?" Finnick asked.

"I'd say that's cocaine." Oscar's deep voice filled the garage, and it took Patrick a second to realize that Finnick had called him in on video call, likely once Simcoe alerted.

Finnick held the phone up toward the heavy bag. "How much?"

"If the bag is even half full," Oscar's disembodied voice said, "depending on what it's cut with, you're looking at ten million on the low end and ninety million dollars on the upper level. You're definitely going to want to bring vice in immediately to collect it."

"I'll stay and handle it," Lucas said. "The rest of you have got a wedding to get to and Darcy's probably not going to make it for another hour or two. She was called in on an emergency shift at work."

Lucas's fiancée was a 911 operator in the Northern end of Toronto. "I'll stay too," Patrick said. "Tristan and I need some quality time, and I'm sure the police are going to have questions for me."

Finnick hesitated. Then he agreed.

"Okay," he said. "Lucas, you're in charge, and you're all welcome to swing by the wedding reception later when you're done."

Patrick had hoped to hug Gemma again before she left and say a proper goodbye. But instead, he stood back and watched as the team called the drug find in and coordinated with Lucas before Finnick, Jackson, Gemma and Caleb hurried out the front door and into their vehicles. Lucas and Michigan went to the garage.

Patrick and Tristan sat on the front step and waited for vice.

The memory of the fleeting kiss Gemma had given him still tingled on his lips. Had it been a kiss goodbye?

"Did Missy really send me a bag of cocaine?" Tristan asked after a long moment.

"It looks like it," Patrick said. "But I think she was just focused on stealing stuff. She didn't realize what she had until those guys were trying to kill her. Maybe she felt bad about what happened to your mom and was trying to make it right in the wrong way. We might never really know why she did what she did. She might not even know."

Tristan nodded, thoughtfully. "People are confusing."

"Yeah," Patrick admitted. "Sometimes."

They lapsed back into silence and Patrick looked out at the snow spread out in front of them, over the trees and down to the faint light on the waterfront of Juniper Cove.

Lord, I've never seen anywhere more beautiful. And I've never wanted to be anywhere else in the world. So, what do I do with the fact everything is tugging me toward something new?

"I think you should marry Gemma." Tristan's voice cut through his thoughts.

"Really?" Patrick blinked and looked down at his son.

"Yeah." Tristan smiled confidently. "She's really nice and helpful. Plus, she didn't complain at all when we had to crawl through the dirty vents."

"And that's a good reason to marry someone?"

"I think so," Tristan said. "Don't you?"

Patrick snorted and hugged his son. "No."

"Then what is?"

Bright white stars shone like twinkling Christmas lights on the velvety black sky above Gemma's head. It was almost midnight and the terrible weather had finally given way to a beautiful winter sky. Behind her in the rustic barn, a local band played, as people sang and clapped their hands, and children ran and played. What had started out as a joyous party for Finnick and Casey's wedding had then morphed into a joint celebration for the fact Tristan was found safe and sound, when Patrick and Tristan had arrived late to the party. People from the community had drifted in and out, as Finnick had announced all friends and family were welcome.

Now Gemma sat on a bench by the water, with her back to the festivities, Simcoe lying in the snow by her feet and her cellphone in her hand, as she tried to find the words to write the hardest letter she'd ever have to write.

Dear Finnick,
I'm so incredibly thankful for the opportunity to be a part of this team. It was literally my life's dream. But recently, I've been wondering if there's another dream I should consider—

Footsteps crunched in the snow behind her. Simcoe woofed happily and her tail thumped the snow.

Who would leave the party to come out here?

"Whoever you are," she called jokingly, "go back to the party! The case is solved! We caught the bad guys! Everything else can wait until after the holidays."

"I wanted to ask if you'd come spend Christmas with us."

Patrick's warm and gentle voice reached her ears. She leaped to her feet and turned, to see him standing in the snow behind her. Her breath caught in her chest. How long had it been since she'd seen him last, across the crowded barn? Twenty minutes? Twenty-five? And yet her heart beat like she hadn't seen him for so long she could barely stand it.

She walked toward him. "What are you doing out here?"

"Looking for you," Patrick admitted. "Is everything okay? What's so important that you're sitting out here on your phone on Christmas Eve?"

She stopped walking, her toes just inches from his, and pressed her lips together.

"I was just writing Finnick a letter asking for a leave of absence," she admitted.

"What?" Patrick's voice rose. "Why would you possibly do that?"

She felt a flush rise to her cheeks and didn't answer. Patrick took her hands, weaved his gloved fingers through hers and tugged her toward him.

"Gemma, why would you ever consider leaving this team?" Patrick asked.

"Because you hate the city." She shrugged. "And I hate the idea of walking away from you."

A smile spread across Patrick's face with a joy that reached his eyes.

"I don't want to lose you either," Patrick said. "I even called Chuck on the drive down, because he's looking for someone to buy an offshoot business of his in Barrie. There are a lot of small towns north of the city."

He looked down at her hands, and his voice grew husky.

"To be honest," he said. "I think I've been using geography as an excuse because I was scared that I'm falling in love with you."

"Me too." She stepped closer until she was practically standing on his toes.

"I figure as long as you promise to be honest with me about your fears," Patrick said, "I promise to be honest about mine, and we face everything that life throws at us head on and together, nothing can tear us apart."

"I love the sound of that," Gemma admitted.

"I love you and I want you by my side."

Happy tears sprung to her eyes. "I'm in love with you too." She pulled her hands from his and wrapped them around his neck. "And I love Tristan."

"Tristan thinks I should marry you," Patrick said. He lifted her up into his arms. "I think I should too."

"Me too."

Her watch beeped announcing that Christmas had arrived and a roar of cheers rose from the party behind them. Gemma laughed and Patrick did too. Then she tilted her head toward him and they sealed it with a kiss before running to tell Tristan and her team the good news.

* * * * *

If you enjoyed Christmas Under Threat,
check out Lucas's story,
Dangerous Arson Trail,
and other stories in the
Unsolved Case Files *series*
by USA TODAY *bestselling author*
Maggie K. Black

Available only from Love Inspired Suspense!
Discover more on LoveInspired.com

Dear Reader,

Today I talked to a friend who'd decided not to put up a Christmas tree in her home this year, because she knew that her three new precious kittens would likely destroy it.

I was suddenly reminded of the Christmas, many years ago back in university, when I offered to be in charge of my church's Christmas tree. To my surprise and delight, I was bequeathed a huge, physical binder of letters written by everyone who'd been in charge of the church tree over the years. They described how they'd decorated the tree—and how it had fit into their understanding of the meaning of Christmas.

Most did one very traditional tree. But one family had put up three small trees. Another had covered the walls with huge garlands instead of a tree. I bought a modest tree and invited everyone in the congregation to make or bring something of theirs from home to hang on it.

Many years later, someone built a Christmas tree out of hockey sticks. That tree was the inspiration for my first holiday book—*Christmas Blackout*.

When I wrote the first draft of this letter, I'd been planning on buying a small live tree from my local hardware store. But yesterday, my teenager unexpectedly brought home an amazing papier-mâché plant from their school production, which we then decorated for Christmas.

Whenever you celebrate and whoever you celebrate with, may your holidays be filled with God's Love and Light. Thank you, as always, for being in my life and sharing this journey with me.

This Christmas, I thank God for you,
Maggie

Get up to 4 Free Books!

We'll send you 2 free books from each series you try PLUS a free Mystery Gift.

FREE Value Over **$25**

Both the **Love Inspired**® and **Love Inspired**® **Suspense** series feature compelling novels filled with inspirational romance, faith, forgiveness and hope.

YES! Please send me 2 FREE novels from the Love Inspired or Love Inspired Suspense series and my FREE gift (gift is worth about $10 retail). After receiving them, if I don't wish to receive any more books, I can return the shipping statement marked "cancel." If I don't cancel, I will receive 6 brand-new Love Inspired Larger-Print books or Love Inspired Suspense Larger-Print books every month and be billed just $7.19 each in the U.S. or $7.99 each in Canada. That is a savings of 20% off the cover price. It's quite a bargain! Shipping and handling is just 50¢ per book in the U.S. and $1.25 per book in Canada.* I understand that accepting the 2 free books and gift places me under no obligation to buy anything. I can always return a shipment and cancel at any time by calling the number below. The free books and gift are mine to keep no matter what I decide.

Choose one:
- ☐ **Love Inspired Larger-Print** (122/322 BPA G36Y)
- ☐ **Love Inspired Suspense Larger-Print** (107/307 BPA G36Y)
- ☐ **Or Try Both!** (122/322 & 107/307 BPA G36Z)

Name (please print)

Address   Apt. #

City   State/Province   Zip/Postal Code

Email: Please check this box ☐ if you would like to receive newsletters and promotional emails from Harlequin Enterprises ULC and its affiliates. You can unsubscribe anytime.

Mail to the Harlequin Reader Service:
IN U.S.A.: P.O. Box 1341, Buffalo, NY 14240-8531
IN CANADA: P.O. Box 603, Fort Erie, Ontario L2A 5X3

Want to explore our other series or interested in ebooks? Visit www.ReaderService.com or call 1-800-873-8635.

---

*Terms and prices subject to change without notice. Prices do not include sales taxes, which will be charged (if applicable) based on your state or country of residence. Canadian residents will be charged applicable taxes. Offer not valid in Quebec. This offer is limited to one order per household. Books received may not be as shown. Not valid for current subscribers to the Love Inspired or Love Inspired Suspense series. All orders subject to approval. Credit or debit balances in a customer's account(s) may be offset by any other outstanding balance owed by or to the customer. Please allow 4 to 6 weeks for delivery. Offer available while quantities last.

Your Privacy—Your information is being collected by Harlequin Enterprises ULC, operating as Harlequin Reader Service. For a complete summary of the information we collect, how we use this information and to whom it is disclosed, please visit our privacy notice located at https://corporate.harlequin.com/privacy-notice. Notice to California Residents – Under California law, you have specific rights to control and access your data. For more information on these rights and how to exercise them, visit https://corporate.harlequin.com/california-privacy. For additional information for residents of other U.S. states that provide their residents with certain rights with respect to personal data, visit https://corporate.harlequin.com/other-state-residents-privacy-rights/.

LIRLIS25